PERCIVAL · LETTERS TO SHANTI

Percival
Letters to Shanti

ART DISTRIBUTION

First published in Sweden in 2002 by
Art Distribution
Askrikegatan 13
SE-115 57 Stockholm
Reprinted with revisions 2003 and 2014

ISBN 978-91-973434-7-3

Designed by the author
Cover design and title-page by Cecilia Frank
Cover photo: Mary Magdalene, painting by Georges de LaTour
    (1593-1652)
Set in 11 on 13 point Bodoni (and Bauer Bodoni)
    by Toivo Alm, Nås, Sweden
Printed by: BoD – Books on Demand, Norderstedt, Germany

The publisher's website and information about books by
Percival in English and in Swedish: www.artdistribution.se
and www.percival.nu
E-mail: artdistributionstudio@gmail.com

Contents

I wish to acknowledge my obligation to friends and particularly to Ana Bodnar for her encouragement and deep and active interest

1994: Looking for a Meeting Place

Inside the Japanese tea-house (Zui-Ki-Tei) in Stockholm.

Dear Shanti

Did you get *Text from the Void* (a booklet)? It was handed over to the receptionist at the City Hotel (Stockholm) the day before your departure. You were not in your room... Did you like the conference? What did you learn, and what do you think about Stockholm?

I wish you were here right now in the sun. It is Midsummer Day. Lovely weather, a clear sky... And the fight against the dragon goes on...

I wonder: Have you seen Jerusalem? Are you on your way back to Canada?

3 July

If I follow my heart – like a Sufi I know in Jerusalem – I must say I feel there is a poet in you too telling us that we ought to wake up... like Briar Rose. – As James Joyce says in his Wake: "For I feel I could near to faint away. Into the deeps. Annamores leep."

You said – on your answering machine – that you would be back on 12 July. – How do you look upon your life now after your journey and the new experiences you've had?

I'm now sitting in the sun, listening to the cooing of pigeons, it's a warm Sunday afternoon by the sea... People's voices from afar... Your voice in my memory...

I am writing, reading *L'amour* (a novel by Marguerite Duras), trying to interpret my dreams, dancing, breathing... and waiting...

Anna Livia Plurabelle is the woman power in Joyce's *Finnegans Wake*. And I know you know somebody by the name of Ana.

9

The Swedish word *ana* means e.g. *divine* – to divine somebody's thoughts, for instance.

But can I guess your thoughts when you have read this letter?

I wish I could.

I look forward to our Day of Rejoicings...

19 July

Yes, I believe in our collaboration... *de jouer... de vivre...* in the Spirit that must impregnate our Time.

The climate in Stockholm has been almost tropical during some weeks. I'm now working in my studio, reading e.g. Albert Camus' novel *Le premier homme*, writing reviews, trying to catch the meaning of this dreamlike existence. It is a great adventure, of course... I live, I act, I read... hoping to meet you again, to stage one (or some) of my plays, to play... to stay... to be with you... Does it make sense? – Yes, I think it does.

I can hear the birds and the noise of the city... I practise yoga, I meditate... and think that we are favoured by Fortune.

How do you look upon your life (your actions) and your freedom of choice?

Jupiter is – as you know – changing just now ... when I write these words. A comet is crashing into Jupiter, and that will perhaps have an influence on the human beings. – What is your opinion?

My awareness tells me that this is the time of transformation and refinement...

I wish you courage, inspiration, and Great Love, given and received.

Warm wind, strong sun, deep breathing, listening to
distant voices, reading your postcard (picture: Sea of
Galilee Centre)... "Let us keep in touch." – And you will
write more, I hope. – Write, live, touch, love, laugh,
dance... What a life it could be straight away...

The desert summer is still going on... Today American
Indians will dance at the Peoples' Museum in Stockholm.

I shall soon give a talk on the Cathars of the Middle
Ages (at my exhibition at Biskops-Arnö)... and I await
your words...

PS. You mentioned Jung on the phone. I've recently read
Emma Jung's and Marie-Louise von Franz' book about
the Fool, the Wise Old Man, the Virgin Maiden, the Waste
Land, etcetera...

Now I look forward to reading the book (about Griffin
and Sabine) that you've sent.

I've just got your letter and your photos. Thanks!

No, I haven't read *The Ever-Present Origin* by Jean
Gebser. Not yet... I'll try to find a copy in Stockholm.

You asked me about your subject: Remembering,
Memory, Healing, Strength...

If you want to gain strength and healing you must be
here, in the present, and – of course – live in truth. What
do you have in mind? Oneness? Concordance?

You could say, We have passed all the borders, left the
prisons behind us, buried the futilities, listened to the
voice of our spirit and found a meeting place.

Have you heard of *hieros gamos* – that is, the sacred
wedding (or marriage)? Or perhaps the Cosmic Wedding,

the Solar Pillar and the Moon Pillar, the wholeness, the true strength?

If your life is a ship – are you the navigator?

And what about the power of the ocean?

I assume you know the novels by Marcel Proust who talked about a sealed memory that could be unsealed and discovered by a certain smell, a certain touch, etc.... The true memory is – according to Proust and Beckett – the memory we don't remember, the memory unspoilt by our superficial time business...

Samuel Beckett says in his book *Proust* that the involuntary memory is more reliable than habit and experience: it reveals the real. But it is "an unruly magician and will not be importuned. It chooses its own time and place for the performance of the miracle."

Finally the curtain rises. You enter... I've been waiting. The play can go on... in the sun...

PS. I might go to Florida in December if I can get a grant. Maybe we could see each other in Florida if you cannot come to Stockholm?

I understand the winter climate in Toronto is rather severe. Even colder than in Stockholm?

The summer has been warmer than it usually is. – I'm writing these words in the morning sun, in the morning wind...

29 August

The Japanese tea-house in Stockholm where we sat together is – as you know – called *Zui-Ki-Tei* (The House of the Promising Light).

It is in this light we shall continue to move in our eternal play.

Yesterday I met a Japanese tea master at the tea-house

and got an invitation to come to his tea-ceremony place in Japan. Have you visited Japan?

When you get these words you will have moved. How do you feel in your new surroundings? Have you also changed your telephone number?

24 September

We could write a book of letters together – or our life together could write the book. Or...?...

I've read your interesting speech about healing in native communities and I've just finished the translation of *Van Gogh le suicidé de la société* by Antonin Artaud (French poet and theatre man) – a book that will be published by a well-known Swedish publisher. I know that you know Artaud. He once said: "I am the man who has best charted his inmost self." – He didn't commit suicide. But what did the society do to him and to Van Gogh... and to a lot of Indian people and to the peoples belonging to the so-called Third and Fourth World... and to artists who are not profitable...?... The struggle of survival goes on at all levels, and I believe that our cooperation is of great importance.

You ask me: "What is your voice?" – I am not sure. Within me there are a lot of voices: the voice of the sun, of the earth, of the wind, of the silence... And of course also: your voice. It's an immense play – our play. I can't overlook it, but I can feel it. Your voice... and mine. Your movements, the importance of being... Here and now... Blue, green, red... And laughs, dance, patience, listening... Can you hear a beach voice, a sea voice, a free voice...?... It is a sunny day today in Stockholm. I'm applying for grants and I imagine that we shall meet again. I would like to listen to your silence, your breath, your sleep, your awakening...

13

Thanks for calling! I can still feel your presence in the room where I usually work – writing, meditating, drumming, listening, reading... I suppose you've read about the ferry tragedy on the open sea (the Baltic). More than 800 people were killed. I was on my way on a ferry to Denmark about 12 hours before it happened.

But instead of thinking about all disasters I now think about our creative collaboration and the meeting-place – Florida? Toronto? California?... Maybe in December or January? I'm awaiting your letter where you'll write about your plans...

Yes, I can hear and feel you in a time outside time... or in a timeless time... where we can rest, talk, and act in the freedom of our spirits. I breathe and you... and the sea, the trees, the air... and perhaps a silent morning full of light... No, I don't doubt, I don't call your presence in question. You are really here and will always continue to be... We are not separated any more. The new time celebration is at hand...

And when we meet I can tell you more... more and more... And you can tell... Eyes, hands, touch... what we meet, what we see and sense... Or: What is the Word: Love, light, spirit, dance...?...

The Korean female shaman Hi-ah Park, I've just seen performing, said: "We must cut through the fear, the fear of not being able to."... etcetera...

To be true: I want to meet you first of all... Then we can make our plans. We could go to California or Sedona...

I will now ask the travel agencies about the possibilities to go to Florida and spend Christmas there. Let us say: Miami Beach. Or do you have any other suggestion?

I hope to raise the amount I need to go there. My applications will be answered around 10 December. But maybe I shall get enough money before that date. Who knows?

Hardships and miseries belong to a past history. I am now on a way that leads to fortune.

Have you ever won anything in a lottery?

Anyhow, I shall give you facts as soon as possible... I could even meet you in Toronto and then we could go together... But Florida (or California?) might be the best place, if there is room before Xmas, when I should like to be with you on a beach or in a fresh forest, on a forest meadow, in an airy wooden house, in a garden not far from the sea... Anywhere where I can listen to your breath, your voice, your thoughts, your silence, your laughs... Your poetry...

This is a new day, a new sunny day... I open a book and read: "completion, reward... travel..."... Do you believe that you can rule your own destiny?

PS. Just now reading about the Virgin Islands (e.g. St John where we could have a yoga retreat together). You can teach me your yoga and I can teach you... But to be able to go to St John I have to win a prize in a lottery or get a lot of money as if by a stroke of magic. Are you skilled in magic?

I feel that the most important thing is our meeting... I know now (by asking a travel agency) that I can fly to Florida (Miami Beach) on Dec. 14, 21 or 24... Do you know somebody there? Where do you intend to stay? I rely on the grant that I hope to get in the middle of Dec. – The tickets are cheaper after 10 Jan. – But will you have time to see me in January or in February?

I'll see what I can do and I agree: "Our time qualities must meet."

I'm reading *Griffin & Sabine* by Nick Bantock: "If you will not join me – then I shall come to you." – But of course I want to join you... Just now I am writing in my studio. It is ten o'clock at night. Last night I saw a samurai film by Akira Kurosawa, a Japanese film director I admire and I suppose you know...

It is rather cold. But no snow in Stockholm so far.

I can almost see our time, our true time, our play time, and no-time... What do you say? – I hope it will be before Xmas...

PS. What did you look like when you were a child?

PPS. You wrote in your last letter:

> *The world of*
>> *Imagination*
> *Hovers at the*
>> *Edge of*
> *Another Dimension*
>> *of Time...*

I like these words. Are they yours? Or mine? Or do they belong to both of us...?...

We have a lot to do together in order to create another Dimension of Time.

No snow as far as I know... At least not here in the middle of Stockholm. But November can be quite snowy... And then the cold winter comes at the end of January as a rule, and a severe winter in a city full of cars and air pollution is far from agreeable.

But by then we might be somewhere else. Somewhere round Christmas we could be at Miami Beach... and then we can go to California if you think that this is a good idea...

No lottery winnings so far... But who knows?

Just imagine we could see the New Year in together and make wishes for our work in progress, for our creative power...

The wind, the golden disc of the sun, your morning's song in a hushed tone... Yes, I can hear it.

PS. As soon as I can buy a ticket I'll let you know. Have you got a driving license?

28 October

You are all the time where I am... But that is not sufficient. You're on the way towards our meeting... And I am... Body, mind, and soul... And true abundance... Reading about Florida: Miccosukee Indian people and the neighbouring Seminole. I saw some traditional Seminole homes in 1991.

I cannot pay the tickets to Florida and California at the moment. But soon I hope.

Everything can be done if you have faith. And we have, I believe.

PS. Enclosing a brochure (a new one) about my books in Swedish. *Time Plays* (not yet published) is also mentioned.

PPS. How about your paintings and drawings? your main things and pain things? your favourite things and play-things?... I trust you're well and happy... Happiness, truth, trust... love.... And our true mission?

I might go to Germany and Denmark at the beginning of December. I shall probably be back in Stockholm about 7 December.

I wish you were here in my studio right now... I'll send you a poem when I've got one from you.

29 October

Soon the Swedes are voting for or against EU (the European Union). Am I not a Swede? – I look upon myself as a world citizen (a citizen of the world). Are you living in Truth?

It is not an easy task – to be true in everyday situations...

I believe I shall get the grant and that we can meet at the end of this year.

The work is going on... Our work... our play in the Great Play... and in my meditation I can hear your voice...

30 October

You want to know what my "intentions are for the U.S."... I've applied for two travel grants. *One*: Florida (California) – Guatemala – Europe. *The other*: a world tour (including Florida and California so that we can meet). *Intentions*: creative work, of course. Our life together is creative. I always try to listen to what the work has to say, to the innermost voice... and I am open to your suggestions... Sanibel might be the right place. But also the Ayurvedic retreat you mentioned. Could we rent a bungalow on the island called Sanibel? The ticket I buy from a travel agency will take me to an hotel in Miami (or Miami Beach). From there we can go by car (or boat?) to Sanibel and spend at least 7-8 days by the sea. Is that a good idea?

To be plain: Had I the money right now I should agree to your first proposal (scheme) and join you in San Francisco. Then we could go to a Buddhist retreat or perhaps to a mountain hut. Have you ever been to the Zen Center, 300 Page Street, San Francisco?

On 10 Dec. I shall get the answer, as I've told you. Time and chance can work miracles... and while we wait, please let me have some more news (facts) about Sanibel and your February possibilities... From prayer to prayer... on this immense River of Life... I am with you and I greet you...

Before I arrive at a final decision I will phone and (or) write...

Our adventure goes on... can we rule our future?

PS. Good morning! Gold morning! God morning! The sun is up. It is shining. Pleasant weather today...

I will try to get some information about Sarasota and Sanibel in Stockholm. I've already found Sarasota on a map. But where is Sanibel?

Have you heard of the Hippocrates Institute (a living food center) in Florida?

12 November

Many thanks for all the snapshots! I like them all, and I believe that you were a serious scholar – even when you were a young girl... But I can also see something else, not just an ordinary child and a schoolgirl. A great inner adventure shines through, and what could not be possible in the light of our future, in the senses and feelings and sensations we are able to discover together in a world that needs our co-acting, our play, our open spirit and mind...

And I agree: "Other things might be possible at the last minute."

I love your spirit, and certainly not only your inner child... Open-heartedness and a magic sense (an extrasensory perception) are qualities I can see that you have.

The leaves are falling, red, brown, yellow... Grey skies... But not always... And the inner sun is shining, the inner dance continues, the dreams... Our song in the quiet of the desert, in the streets, the forests... on the mountains... By the way: Do you have mountains in your immediate neighbourhood?

I am still reading *Le premier homme* by Camus, writing now and then, dancing sometimes, meeting people... Now looking into your eyes seeing your inner child and talking to that child...

Can I answer your questions: "How were you as a child? Where is the child in you?" – I imagine you can guess... when we meet...

27 November

Imagine you exist somewhere on this earth and that I can write to you, talk to you, meet you...

Imagine we are together healing the earth and our own lives...

Imagine we are in a forest full of firs or in a log-cabin by the fire...

Imagine we are sitting by the fire and you ask me something and I say, Yes...

Imagine...

And realize...

And open up and speak... and sing... and dance... and listen to the waves...

"Past now pulls"... I quote *Finnegans Wake* and say: You must not hesitate. It is time to revise the opinion of

Time, life, nations, history... And what do you think about the masculine and the feminine, about our sacred (secret?) mission...?...

Tell me something about your view of life and your life-work. Do you have guides and a guiding-star?

PS. I've today (28 November 1994) received information from the Lee County Visitor and Convention Bureau in Florida. Yes, it might be the right place... I mean: Sanibel. Maybe we could rent a cottage: one of the Sanibel Cottages, 2341 West Gulf Drive, Sanibel Island, FL 33957? – A meditation cottage where we can live and create our new reality...?...

I will meditate on this prospect.

10 December

I like your poems: about the bridge and the Black Madonna... "and I did dream you after all..."

Some days ago (in Denmark) I saw a sky that had a shade of apricot and I saw a red sun rise between the wings of wind power stations close to the sea.

Now I am in Stockholm and it is grey and it is raining and it is rather quiet. I am reading about the Mitchell's Sand Castles, e.g. the bungalows "Pelican" and "Coquina & Sea Grape".

The retreat site Rasayana Cove is also a good place to stay at, to relax and find the inner serenity.

We can come to a decision when I've got the answer I've told you about. I hope I shall know before 15 December.

The gypsy in me wants to meet the gypsy in you, and of course: in this ascension time our creative imagination can form a new reality – a new-born awareness of standing with our feet on the ground (as you write) and "seeing spirit in the trees". Spirit and spirits.

I love your song that I can hear in my deep meditation. There – in your song – I feel at home. I mean: In the stream (the aura) of (from) your body, mind, and soul...

Stockholm, 18 December

Do you remember *Zui-Ki-Tei* – our first place of meeting?

Where is the next place? – Fort Lauderdale on 3 February 1995? I shall arrive at the airport at eight o'clock (19.55) p.m.

On 4 February we could go to Sanibel and rent a cottage ("Pelican" or "Coquina") for a week. Then I'll go back to Europe by Icelandair from Fort Lauderdale on 11 February 6.20 p.m. (18.20).

And you will go back to Toronto. And then we can see each other in Stockholm.

All this can become a reality...

PS. Now I write again. To you. For you. For our time together on this planet, a playful time, a time of love, a fortunate time...

You are always welcome to my studio in Stockholm.

What do you think about 1995? Our year! our free-hearted year! Our personal consciousness will blend with the universe...?...

I want to listen to your breath and your silence... to talk with you without talking... *Together* we can heal the waste land.

19 December

What a great adventure we have initiated!

What does the Universe want us to do in the coming chapters?

Are we written or do we write? What about the free will?

I wrote that I intended to go to Florida on 3 February, but now I know that Icelandair is fully booked on that day.

An Art Distribution-collaborator (who has got a driving licence) is interested in going to the Ayurvedic Centre – Rasayana Cove – in Florida on 1 February, and I know it is possible to buy "fly & drive tickets" from Stockholm. Then I could pick you up in Fort Lauderdale or in Miami Beach and we could go together to Sanibel.

I would really like to treat you to a Sanibel week and everything else... Anything you could imagine. And maybe one day...

We can speak on the phone before you go to California.

When you celebrate our New Year in California I will make an inner space travel and be together with you on a cosmic level. The holiness, our sacred wholeness, belongs to our play... I quote some of your words:

"The bridge is
the heart
that connects
and makes whole"
our land
that has been laid
waste
but soon will flower.

31 December

I have got your last letter where you suggest we go to Sarasota... And "a less pricey cottage" in the neighbourhood of Sarasota might be the right place for our meeting (in February). You are closer to this reality and can investigate and find out...

You are a real twin soul, I mean: you are Gemini, fire and air and some earth...

Of course there is also fire in me, a solar fire, and the other elements, the fury of the elements and the stillness, the still point in a universe full of creative movements. And in that still point I can feel you, I can meet you, I can be with you...

Our year – 1995 – is coming closer... The Buddhist calendar says: "All will be bountiful."

What if we could start to rule our own stars and ask our helping spirits to guide us and protect us in our creative work, in our union... and prepare the true place for our cosmic play?... Can you follow me?

We are on the stage and a stage voice says: The dream that we are must be played and lived with all senses open and receptive... We are moving towards a higher awareness, and together we can see and feel more than what I can now see and feel here in Stockholm. And you are far away, maybe on Mt. Madonna. Is the Black Madonna in you a voice I can hear in this silence before everything turns... and the new year, the new Cosmic Year, is born...?...

Sand, feet, waves, and a dance... Is it your dance I can see? your song I can hear? Yes, I agree with you: "the earth and the sky need each other in order to create warmth and life."

Soon I will see the fireworks, and I am already where you are in my thoughts. Where else could I be?

PS. 2 January 1995. It is snowing.

24

1995: Year of Initiation

The secret key of the universe is hidden in the golden
mind within us revealing its truth when the Kingdom of
Death is gone.

Dear Shanti

Winter, snow, white days, cold air, dark people... and
sometimes the sun and bright colours, black trees and red
houses...

Today I've been reading *Le Coeur d'Amour Epris*.
Perhaps you have heard of René, king and poet, who in a
magical night is involved in an adventurous journey, a
quest for Sweet Grace.

I wish we were together somewhere in Florida... but not
in the flooded area of California.

I've recently applied for a new grant, and I am hopeful.
I hope you will send me some data and news about Sarasota, etcetera.

You said in your letter of 19 Dec.: "I may have to wait
until later in February or even early March." – What do
you say now?

You also write: "Not enough earth and one flies here
and there." – But if we fly together and stand on the
earth together and create a new world together...?...

I think we need to give each other energy, and I believe
we could create (and play) a ritual play in order to heal
humanity...

Just now: Silence, winter, night, cold, snow, sleep... The
news talks about the war the Russians are engaged in...
And all the victims... and all the people on the run... in
this nuclear power age.

But I am hopeful... And I hope that we shall meet in
February...

We are all waiting for the descending of the Holy Spirit,
aren't we?

Or are we just slaves to fashion and nothing more?

Low-spiritedness is at least not ruling my work and my
life.

O Lady bright, thou art aware of all my thoughts...

and I now invite you to a solar initiation time and a solar initiation work.

Maybe we could get an invitation to Mérida, Chichén Itzá, and Uxmal.

In performing my solar initiation as the Red Knight I would need Queen Blue in order to create a blessing wholeness.

I really hope we shall be invited.

A whole world is in need of a true solar initiation.

Naturally enough I am – as you are – interested in being close to a sunny sea and intelligent dolphins.

But I don't think – as I've told you – that we have to go to the Bahamas just now...

We can discover Florida's west coast and the "spirit in the trees, and the mind and the hearts, the song of shadows, and of softness and of wetness, and of earth" (as you've written in one of your "Madonna-poems").

PS. Shall we meet in St Petersburg or in Tampa or...?...

Days Inn, Tampa, Florida, 21 February

We have been together, and I *miss* you, but I know that you are full of happiness... And all that happens to you is in the deepest sense happiness. To think of that makes me happy... Just now on my way to St Petersburg and Clearwater Beach.

In my past life I've looked upon myself as a Lion (a Leo-man). Now I feel more like an Aquarius being...

It's a new Star time we are living in... and my true birth is coming closer...

My best wishes for your creative writing. I like your poetry... and you are on the whole a true poem in progress...

"It's outrageous" – as you used to say –, outrageous and gracious, our time here on earth.

PS. 21 February 1995

> I am in Tampa on the beach.
> No, I don't have a mobile telephone on the beach.
> We've just talked, and we know we can talk.
> We have danced and we know we can dance.
> (You know, we should have danced more!)
> We should go on a dancing-trip.
> We were on fire all the time, a world on fire...
> *Sagebrush*, you said. – Yes, I used to use that myself...
> You told me you are a priestess now.
> Yes, it's rather hot, I am sitting here in the shadow
> After our conversation over the phone.
> I have met Queen Blue.
> From now on I am living like a king.
> Having met the Queen
> I want to continue to live like a King.

27 February

I have got your poems, and I like them, I can feel the truth in them... And you know that the Red Knight is a name used during a certain period, the quest period, an uncertain time when the true castle is hidden... But that time is almost over. It is not enough to follow your head or your heart or your will and desire. You must be whole. The grace of your true nature must take over, and that grace is greeting you – who no longer are the sleeping Briar Rose.

29

The birth is approaching, and the love of Sophia belongs to our new time, a time we have inaugurated... I've done a lot of mistakes when I just followed my head; I've done mistakes following my heart or my will or my desire... and my spontaneity... But could I have acted otherwise? Didn't I have to do what I did? Were not all my acts a part of the quest? – I am not sure.

It is not easy to become a true human being. It might be easier to be a god or a goddess. Then you can go on joking, dancing, laughing... and behave as if mankind were a disaster, an experiment that has a time-limit, a plaything to be used in a creation not even the gods or the goddesses understand... But the Kingdom of Dawn is coming closer; the Queendom of Dawn is coming closer... the healing of the wound is coming closer...

And I see that you are blessed and I bless you...

We have played and lived and created the second chapter. The third one – The Chapter of Dawn – is opening its Gate.

Please tell me something about your daily work, the home you have, and our next meeting place...

Northern Europe, 2 March

The Sun is strong. It is almost spring. It is 14 degrees above zero...

How do you feel? Do you want to write the next chapter...?... Or at least the first half of it?

Do you think that our book (novel, letters?) will have seven chapters? Will it be a fairy-tale with a happy end? Who can tell? The work goes on... in the shade, in the sun... And who can judge? Who is right? who is wrong?

Your soul might know. It tells you how to act rightly. Your heart soul... is a good writer. I believe it can find the true opening words of the third chapter.

30

Our story is not a small story. It belongs to the world.

And now we have to move up a little higher... I can feel the strength of your time presence. Yes, you are here.

Hommage à Shanti!

Let us play *à la belle étoile!*

PS. I don't know yet if I can go to Mexico at the vernal equinox experiencing the Mayan Solar Initiation.

PPS. There are (as you probably know) a lot of books about the Red Knight – medieval books and books written in our own time (e.g. by Emma Jung and Marie-Louise von Franz).

Even in India (and in Sri Lanka) and among the Indians (e.g. Maya and Hopi) there are legends (myths) about the Red Knight. – But we are of course creating a new story, a new history... Or: Our life...

Europe, Easter 1995

White Caribbean beach (Mexico), high fever, palms, snakes, and the New World's big cat, the jaguar, threatened by deforestation and poaching. The fever, the immense light, the immense sea that finally baptized me... Then the old world was almost gone, just a heap of ashes... I recall how I stood up and went to Tulum, the Place of Dawn, the Place of Awakening, and when I was lying on the ground close to a temple I heard a tone coming from nowhere filling all the space... I felt that the sky was holding its breath and that the flowers of the jungle were waiting for the rain to fall... It was no-time... What is time to me anyhow?... It was just the beginning... Chase and be chased... No, I am nowhere... And yet I am here, beside the temple in a Maya jungle where I could hear the keel-billed toucan, where I saw the pigs and the

31

hens, where I talked to the beggar children who asked me for pesos I didn't have... Now and then I could feel your presence in a time without time...

Yes, I celebrate the light each day, and I believe that I am living on a planet called Earth, but I am not sure... You told me on the phone that you felt "pissed-off", and that is at least something... It is Easter and Passover (God will not smite the first-born in the houses where we live) and Pâques (in Swedish: påsk)... I think that James Joyce calls it "Eatster" in his *Finnegans Wake*...

Well, we really have a lot to do, and you are welcome to Europe that needs to be turned on by your spirit...

Easter Day 1995

Thanks for calling! – You want me to tell you more about my Yucatán experience. I could of course say something extra about what happened during the Mayan Solar Initiation, I mean the ritual I performed on the steps of a solar temple in Uxmal, Mexico, the choir I created... but now... I don't know... Yes, I remember a man called Luis who said he was a spiritual seeker and a founder of the Academia Mexicana de Medicina Alternativa (Cancún).

He came up to me after my ritual in front of the solar temple and I told him a few things, something about the freedom you need when the soul awakens to creation... Yes, he understood, and later we saw a young man kneeling in front of an altar with the Mayan shaman Hunbatz Men behind him – a shaman who gave him an initiation with certain gestures and ancient Mayan incantations... And afterwards, when this man "woke up", the nature he felt and saw was newly born: the song of a bird, the little wind in a shrub, the silent breath of the air... It was at the beginning of the afternoon. Time was taking its first steps... Almost all the others had gone to their lunch. The interspaces talked, the male and the female voices had mingled, and now: silence...

And AUM Shanti, Shanti, Shanti...

No, I am not here... I am still in Yucatán or in Florida with you. Or somewhere else... Perhaps we are living and working together in New Mexico? Perhaps our true story is about to start?... The spring is here, the birds (not many) are singing – at least in the forest (I hope). But sometimes the silence is alarming, and the lack of life makes me afraid... Where are all the living souls, where are all the courageous people who refuse to obey the slave-drivers and the nature killers and the joy killers?

Your open heart is what the world needs, your true words, and your joyfulness... You are a performer, a poet, a savant, a free spirit... And I know that you can play and laugh and dance and sing and run a house, and so on...

At present I'm looking at a photo of a Mot-Mot (a bird) perched on a limb of a flamboyant tree with date palm seed...

We need living sources, living forests, living words, living love, living spirit... And I am dreaming of our reunion in this silent spring afternoon. The sky is cloudy, the trees are still without leaves, crocuses (blue) can be seen in front of the house where I am living, and I should like to know more about your everyday life. We are preparing ourselves for a new meeting...

Solar Earth wishes

PS. The proof-reading goes on... My next novel in Swedish – *The New Man's History. The Sign of Lazarus* – will be published by Carlssons in August (or September) this year. It is a miracle book – full of secret messages.

It is late at night, I've spoken to you on the phone, I've read your letters, your wonderful poem called "Shoulder Nectar/ Lion Moon" and I will do my best to speak "with open heart" – according to your wish. I think you know what I feel, and I agree with you when you write: "I would like to share with you a mystical adventure"... So, here we are, on this earth, you in Canada (or maybe in Mexico) and I in Europe... I have some friends in Stockholm, yes... Or rather: work-mates... And the struggle for survival goes on. But I admit: there is always a lot of creative happiness in my work as a writer... And as I have told you: I am being written... Time is changing. New light is giving the stage a warmer colour, and there you are – "not a shadow/ but a real palm girl".

Yes, I can realize that, and I can sense an adventure that will give our life (our lives) an altogether different meaning.

You ask: "Who is Parzival's shadow and fool? Who is always forgotten when Parzival is there, in the centre stage?" Have you read Wolfram von Eschenbach's book *Parzival*?

I think you know the answer better than I do, or perhaps there is an answer in my play *The Kingdom of Man* and in the novel I will publish this year... But not the whole answer. I can only give this answer when we are together, when we live together, when I can hear your breath and inhale the presence of your soul, mind, and body...

Now I am just waiting for the door to open, for your entrance, for the play to begin, for the show to start, for our silent laughter on the beach, under a palm, on a mountain, in a morning wind full of a sweet fragrance... Yes, the summer is approaching, and we must meet...

If you go to Mexico you might be able to meet Hunbatz Men, but he is – as you know – very busy. I think you would like him. He is open-minded and open-hearted, and his knowledge about his own Mayan sun and moon culture is very deep.

I wrote in a notebook:

"After 520 years of silence and darkness the Itzá-Maya-people of Yucatán – at least some representatives of that people – have chosen to break the silence and declare a new solar era opened. That is what happened at the Spring Equinox 1995 when people from all over the world made celebrations and ceremonies at some sacred sites: Dzibilchaltún, Chichén Itzá, and Uxmal. They partook in ceremonies that were partly prepared by the Mayan shaman Hunbatz Men, and partly created on the spot. My cosmic and solar Time Opening Rite was in this context a surprise – performed on the stairs of a Solar Temple (Solar House) in Uxmal... I really hope that the Mayan people soon will be able to stage their own rites at their ceremonial places, such as Uxmal and Chichén Itzá..."

The Mayans need their stages back, and I need my stages... Both are occupied by the Enemy. And I can assure you: My time on the battlefields of Europe (including Sweden) has not been an easy one... But I know: Time is changing, and you are finally here...

Solar greetings on the top of a pyramid in Uxmal and the author in front of Quetzalcoatl's pyramid in Chichén Itzá, Mexico.

Partakers of the Solar Initiation (1995)
watching the Solar Serpent.

Resurrection morning in Tulum, Mexico, April 1995.

Yes, you are a real miracle and together we can create a miracle time...

The summer is here and my thoughts are where you are... There is a Peace in Mind Festival in Stockholm, but I am not there. I have other things to do. I will walk in the sun, do my own shaman trips, imagine a new theatre world, stages where I will stage my plays, gardens where we can dance, an island where we can live, a mountain... a lake, a river, a sea...

And where have you been all this time, all these ages without true feelings, without true creation, without true creative power...?... No, the true world has not yet started to exist, but I now have a feeling of a fuller existence than we have hitherto known, a you-and-me-existence, a multidimensional life with sharp senses full of creative skill and ability, a waking-up-movement, a birth dance, a song play, a new ray, a royal reunion day...

It is Whitsuntide, the time of the white Sun, first the Eve and then the Day, and I can see you as a birthday child receiving presents in a green garden in a time when Heaven and Earth finally are starting to understand each other...

And I am there, of course, yes, I am there in the air that surrounds you and I wish you many birthdays and a real BIRTH DAY...

10 June

You are raising yourself, you are raising the earth, you lift it up, you open the heavens, the total presence is there, you can free what is imprisoned, you can set anybody free, the maiden petrified with horror, yes, time itself... And the holy pyramid (in Uxmal) is suddenly turned into a theatre, where a light performance is performed, a ballet drama – like in the ancient days...

But the spirit is changed, there is no bloody sacrifice any more, no people killed, no war cry...

This is just a beginning of a much bigger drama that soon will be staged when the minds of the humans have been prepared enough. A renascent life will start, a *fincarnate* life as Joyce writes, and all the heavy burdens will belong to a past history...

Do you like the scent of lilac?

Tell me about your secret dreams and your true mission on earth!

It is a silent day and the sky has been overcast... But now the sun has returned...

24 June

You asked me about Tantra. That is a long story. I suggest you read the books by Ajit Mookerjee – e.g. *Tantra Asana – a way to self-realization* (published by Ravi Kumar) or *The Art of Tantra* by Philip Rawson (Thames and Hudson, London) or *Tibetan Yoga and Secret Doctrines* (Edited by W.Y. Evans-Wentz, Oxford University Press) or *The Awakening of Kundalini* by Gopi Krishna (E.P. Dutton & Co., New York) or... Well, as I said, it's a long story, it will never end, and we are in it, this story, you and me and the whole world and our true co-creation and the deep blue, the sea blue, the sky... our senses like an albatross sailing above the clouds, and at the same time mastering the emotions on the earth plane.

It is Midsummer. People are celebrating the pale blue Midsummer Night. For the moment I am listening to Enigma's *The Cross of Changes*... and time will not end. We simply have to move up a little higher so that we can laugh and dance and enjoy our life... No use to be a

recluse or carry a heavy burden... "Life is not a burden,"
as your master has said... And perhaps we shall find the
key so that we can open the door and really see and hear
and sense our whole story without end...

PS. Tantra is a way of getting to know your body and not
run away from it. You should listen to it and try to figure
out what it has to say. It needs a lot of care and good
nourishment, but that is not all... There are subtle
realities which are even more important than the food
you eat, an exchange of energies for example and a poetic
and playful outlook on things. And of course you know
the interplay between male and female energies...

But there is more to be discovered. Most of us are in a
junior school in this, and now people are waiting for the
photon belt to change them. I suppose you've heard talks
about becoming a galactic human and the coming earth
changes...

I don't know. What is a true human (being)?

The book *The Celestine Prophecy* is far from great art,
but it might be a valuable guidebook in certain cases.
What do you say to that?

And where do we meet?

I should need some Nobel Prize money right now!

12 July 1995. Or: a time without time

X Marks the Spot

It is late. The reawakening is at hand.
A king, a night, a light
Filling the space...
We have not much to say, no place
Of Origin, no end, no beginning...

Or do we master our destiny without
Knowing our future?
Love, remembrance, fortunes,
A lucky room for ever,
And now a new morning is here
In this soul-sleeping summer-city
Where the only true reality is my dreams...
And a lack of a fortune to be able to do
What I want...

Sometimes I feel I ought to write as Joyce writes in his
Finnegans Wake, that is, mix a lot of tongues... "You have
eaden fruit. Say whuit. You have snakked mid a fish. Telle
whish."

Tell a wish, tell me...

Who is free, who has no sin, who is in a heavenly mood,
who does never brood over this and that, who has a mind
full of gold and sun in this funny time?... Or rather:
strange time...

The magpies are croaking in the lindens (the lime-trees)
in the morning sun...

It is a new day, and I wonder: What do you have to say?

You know the haves and the have-nots... What a have!
No, I don't want to belong to this lot. And I already have
a lot. Yes, we at least have a lot of freedom in our mind.
And we can create a new time...

You are in California sharpening your senses, I
believe...

27 July

No, I am not going wooing,
I am not a wooer on the spree,
no, I am not going on a buying spree,
I am free and maybe astute,

my roots are growing in the soil
of eternity...

And now it is a warm sunny day. I have got your letter
from the Zen Mountain Center, and you know that I
appreciate the Zen Buddhist meditation as much as you
do. Still I am glad that you are a yogini and a poet and a
charming woman full of wit and spirit. I wish I could meet
you every day in order to develop our play in Time, our
Time Play...

Sometimes you are red, sometimes blue... And perhaps
you can read the stars. What do they tell you? In your
thesis you write: "In this vision, the world flows out of the
sacred centre and everything falls into place around it."

21 August

Morning again, play time, time's voice whispering, where
is all the dust coming from, strong voices singing, drilling-
machines can be heard, streets are being repaired...

Every morning at sunrise magpies visit my balcony, I
usually wake up when I hear their harsh chattering
voices. The Water Festival is over, the sun is still strong,
and some people do have a heart...

Can you feel the earth changes, the tongue of the water,
the tongue in your mouth, the tongue of our time?

Everywhere they talk about personalities; they say, He
has a personality, She has... But what is personality, what
is spirit, the Holy Ghost, life?

I breathe in the world of spirits, in the green woods, on
the sea, in the cities... But it is sometimes hard to breathe
in a city, to really inspire, to feel at home... to be, to let
go... to laugh and dance and sing... and behave as a true
creation ought to behave... But where is the true
creation? Have we lost it? The true feeling, the sense of

touch, the golden cup and the morning drink...?...
And now silence... and all obligations knocking at the
door... It is the time of action, an action in the sun...

PS. Thanks for the article about the guerrillas in
Kashmir and my young Norwegian friend Hans Christian
Ostrø, who had just started working on his new Catharsis
Theatre. He was on his way to the holy Amarnath Cave
when he was captured by so-called guerrillas (terrorists).

20 September

You know that I don't write stories, no, no stories... But
the life in me writes me. And here I am, in Sweden, in
Stockholm, in Europe... waiting for a possibility to
leave... Would Mars suit me? No. I don't think so. A life
with you on a Caribbean island wouldn't be too bad...
How do you feel about that?

What makes you happy? to write? to dance? to sing? to
be loved? to love...?...

Now I remember a sentence from a science fiction film I
saw at the beginning of this year: "A storm will come, our
storm, and when it comes it will shake the Universe."

Perhaps it is coming soon. And this is the silence before
the storm. I don't know...

Is life an ordeal we are passing through?

What Silence is this? "The earth might be uninhabited"
as Krapp says in *Krapp's Last Tape* – a play by Samuel
Beckett.

I need some nature, some wind, a sunny beach, drums,
and dancing people... And of course: a theatre with many
stages.

You want me to start to write a story... and you never
know... Who can tell, the story might come... But now I
am waiting for a new sign in my life, a new sign, a new

sun, a new life spiral... And what is your opinion about the French nuclear bomb tests?

I really feel like I want to change planet and solar system... The earth-dwellers are getting on my nerves. But there are exceptions, and you are one of them... More news later on when I feel more at home.

29 September

No, Mars is not my place. Is this earth my home? I wonder.

Do you love to be in the great outdoors? Do you love reproductions, replicas, nostalgic accessories, etc.? do you... love?

Time to laugh, time to sing, time to be, to listen, to be silent... to create new words, or Maya words: *Imix... Ixim... Kin...* Shop the world, a world shop... I am sitting... No... Wait at the gateways, I will come, don't worry, sooner or later... I just have to find the true knights, the true damsels, the true... I just have to before... No, I will not succumb, I will move towards the procession on the way to Eternity, all dressed in white... Yes, I know I shall reach them... Yes, just wait at the gateways, I will return with the right knights, who are full of spirit and know how to fight without killing anybody... Just wait by the gateways, keep a sharp eye on what is going on... Prepare the feast, the hall, the candelabras... Keep watch, I'll be back, on horseback or on foot... Create a ring in the hall in the middle of the castle, light the candelabras when you can see me coming together with all the white knights, tell the damsels to join the feast and don't forget the Virgin Queen... The darkness is falling, the wind is sighing in the trees, the moon is hunting through the clouds, children are dancing on the moor; mother is gone, is gone...

Was denkst Du? Ich denke nicht. Ich will ein Märchen erzählen... a tale about my way back home to the golden city, about the dark streets, the dark trees, the gloomy skies, the people of this world, the life I can see when the mist is lifting...

My umbrella is laughing in my dream, I don't walk on ice, I don't scream... What are they talking about in the marshland, I'm trying to listen, there is something in the wind, but I'm not lost... I can see the white procession on the move towards eternity and perhaps one day...

11 November

This is a time of prayfulness, of playfulness, but the deep sorrow has not yet parted from our time ship, the fight for survival is a reality everywhere...

We need long pauses, a power recharching, a playful healing where we can forget about time and obligations...

I don't know really what is happening... People are talking about the Phoenix Gate that we are now passing through burning off old karma... or all karma...

Why are we here after all? To toil like slaves, to dream of a paradise, to mount a play...?... to write a poem, to live a poem, to be...?...

An ordinary day at five o'clock in the afternoon in a street called the Craftsman Street (in Stockholm): autumn darkness, lots of light, nice small shops, lots of people, heavy trucks, noises, roaring, busses, cars, stinking air... can hardly breathe, trying to keep on a conversation, be polite, be somebody in a body, be on earth, be here, talk like a human being, worship man-kind, at least say something funny, conjuring up a new heaven and a new earth, praying for the angels to descend and for the minds to open to reality, remembering the pine-forest air, the scent of pine-trees,

the silent forest, the roaring sea, you and me, the flying
albatross, the sound of a flute, the brute force, the World,
the Justice, the Judgement...

We are just now passing through the Phoenix Gate and
the Star Gate... Heavenly voices can be heard, and I look
forward to the true fulfilment of our earth mission...
Hoping to stage my plays, to publish books in English and
compose holy and healing sounds, wave music, a New-
Era-music regenerating sleepy minds and bodies on this
sleeping Earth Stage.

> The eyes are dreaming,
> Hesitating... asking:
> Must we burn all our
> Old *karma* so that we
> Can play and not judge
> In this world full of judges?

1996: Year of Silence and Celebration

From the author's studio.

Dear Shanti

You are there, I am here. I wish I were somewhere else. In
a desert with you or on a sunny beach... This snow and
this winter and all these cold minds don't suit me... You
wrote something about "a barrier melted"... and "half of
a pyramid"... I wish I knew the story behind... But as it is
now I know nothing because of this dead city and a
culture that is completely foreign to me... I am dreaming
of wild dances, of le Mont d'Or, of the Fuerteventura
desert I've just visited, of the restaurant, no, the bar
Waikiki Beach and a troubadour singing: "The answer,
my friend, is blowing in the wind, the answer is blowing
in the wind..."...

Can I say I've chosen the wrong planet or the wrong
civilization or the wrong time? Is the lack of money
governing my life? Would I live on a Canary island or in
New Mexico or in the Bermudas or on some Caribbean
island... if I had enough means?... I don't know... It may
well be I would buy a house on some Canadian mountain
(a sacred mountain) and invite you to come and visit me...

Life is a very strange invention or riddle or play... Now
I don't know if I can go to Yucatán in March, probably I
have to stay in Stockholm... Anyhow, the solar revolution
is growing in new-born souls and I look forward to
encountering the sacred through my coming life
experience...

Easter 1996

What a life it could be right away! Say a resurrection of
everybody! Isn't this world a tomb? How many can really
enjoy their stay on earth? No, I don't mean we should

arrange a lot of cocktail parties but why not dance in the streets and stop paying all these destructive people who have turned the world into a horrifying and money-obsessed mess... By the way, have you seen *Underground* – a film by Emir Kusturica? I think you would like it, and I really hope we could meet and start to co-create... in this world that has been occupied by some strange aliens who have no real compassion in their life and treat soul, spirit, and body like thralls... Well, you find the slave-trade everywhere... And here I am, almost pinioned in a kind of prison – in an urban society that is in need of more spirit, culture, joy, play, fun...?... Naturally I admit you can find exceptions, but they are rare... Sometimes I am drumming, sometimes I am speaking to listeners, sometimes I am greeting the sun... waiting for an inner dawn to break, a break-through, an enlighted encounter... a lifting of the veil, light masters opening new stages, new lines, new channels...

From here to eternity... I know we ought to *re-Joyce*; the spring light is getting stronger, you will soon go to California, and I will find my way out of the deep, dark forest... What do you create, what do you think...?... Do you feel like a million dollars?

11 April

I wrote that the world seems to be occupied by some strange beings calling themselves humans... And to tell you the truth...: Who has the nerve to say no to all this forgery? Where is there a true culture, a true heart, a wise man, a holy spirit?

Our civilization has failed, the culture is dead, the civilized man has lost his wit; he cannot even breathe... And I don't know what to do... in a prison where nobody cares...

Joyce writes: "Lok! A shaft of shivery in the act..." New age people are talking about ascension and the photon belt... Not only the senses, the whole body will change, they say... And soon... At the end of the year there will be mass landings; some say at the beginning of the fall. They talk about friendly aliens coming to save us or to teach us something. – Will they understand my poetry? I wonder. – Will they understand man's history, man's soul history? And the language of nature, the plant life, the animals, the angels? Or are they angels? Have you ever seen an angel? Have you understood the tongue of the angels?

Stockholm is quite a small ant-hill, Toronto is bigger... But where is the beauty, the true beauty that is a soul ascension, a nature and art world we need? The creation goes on, and we are responsible...

27 May

Thanks for your news about California!

You told me about the cold spring in Toronto. Stockholm has also been cold this spring... I wish I could travel backwards through time in a boat of gold, maybe on the Heavenly Nile where I can look for a new life that must be hiding somewhere in our past history... Now the wind is blowing, the sea is breathing, the tongues are heard and it is getting brighter and brighter... Soon it is play time, world time, star time... And where are you? On a quest? In the city, on a mountain, in a river valley...?... trying to grasp our time's wisdom and knowledge...?... And what about all these zombies, killers, money-bags, misers... and all the knights errant without shelter, without home, without love...?...

You seem to be working a lot, eating very simple vegetarian food (I suppose) and really enjoying your dream- time and your psychospiritual counselling... You

wrote that you are happy in your heart. Am I happy? I
don't know. I think I could be happier – e.g. staging one
of my plays or meditating with you on a sunny and
warm beach, listening to the sea in a no-time-full-of-life-
existence...

15 July

I was really glad to receive your comforting words: "Be
well & happy & may your heart find its home." – You
seem to know me. No home so far. – An outsider, a Gypsy
(a Romany)? Yes, in a way... And you know that I am a
desert man and that I love the sea and tropical islands...

The summer is enjoyable here in Stockholm.

At the beginning of August I shall give a talk on man,
the French poet Saint-John Perse, the elements, and the
creative power... during Stockholm's Water Festival.
Saint-John Perse was a poet who really understood the
powers of nature: the wind, the sea, the snow, the rain,
the storm... In his epic poem *Vents* (Winds) he writes:
"Car c'est de l'homme qu'il s'agit, dans sa présence
humaine; et d'un agrandissement de l'œil aux plus hautes
mers intérieures." (Because it's man that matters, in his
human presence; and the widening of the eye towards the
highest inner seas.)

Next month I'll start to organize a festival celebrating
Artaud's centenary. Like Perse he is a poet whose
wordings are creating a time beyond the Last Judgement.

I'll never forget the Sanibel Island-time with you. When
do we meet again? – That's the question.

The dark clouds go past, the sun shines again, and you
are like a princess in a fairyland – far, far away...

You are also a healer and a shaman... But do you
dance, do you sing, do you wait for a message, a propo-
sition, a mission, an invitation...?... Or a fortune and a
new adventure?

54

Outside the Grand Masters' Palace, Rhodes.

Strong sun, wild sea, clear sky, blue time, life is playing...
Voices filling the air... This is the island of Helios, and I
feel at home... Yoga exercises on the beach, reading,
writing, and soon joining an international writers'
meeting... and a performance and a dinner at a medieval
castle, the Grand Masters' Palace.

What do you think: Do we create our own time? – What
is time, anyhow? Have you now started to sculpt your
own time?

Enclosing a poem written yesterday:

> The body of Man
> Is far from fully created.
> It is at the utmost
> An embryo in the ocean of Creation
> Where the consciousness of Man
> Is rolling to and fro
> Without having found a true foothold...
> We are still living in a Death Land
> And not in a sun that gives us deliverance.
> Our true origination
> Is waiting for its dawn.

27 October

Yesterday I saw the play *The Seven Streams of the River
Ota* by Robert Lepage. I don't know what to say. Of
course: entertaining, full of mirth and sorrow, irony,
satire... and slapstick in a beautiful wrapping...

But I have the feeling: Everybody is asleep, the whole
history, and especially some parts of the world where a
ruthless exploitation is going on. And I cannot talk to

anybody... I just have to behave as if I could enjoy certain people's efforts to destroy what man used to call soul or living spirit or creative freedom of the innermost being... But there are perhaps oases hiding somewhere in this immense desert... Yes, I must say I have known a few living rebellious spirits in this part of the world, but they have already passed the border and sometimes I don't see much light with the exception of my dreams where I am able to meet shadows who seem to understand the true gifts of our destiny...

Winter and rough weather will come and I don't see any reason for me to stay in this cold country if I can't find a suitable stage for my plays and open hearts for my words... But I am not pessimistic and not a mystic. I want to live here and now and use the full range of my capacity. The work goes on... We are acting our lives to the best of our ability. I am here... You are there... Anybody could be anywhere... And the bodies need to be taken care of, perhaps reshaped and uplifted before it is too late to act and the play is over. I've heard it on the radio, I've seen it on TV, I've read it in *Time*... There are splashes of hope, the ocean is still a living organism... We can start grass-roots movements on a global scale...

And here I am, in my room, at my desk, in my kitchen... in the air of this planet... and probably in some way living a protected albeit surpressed life in a corner of a world-stage where people are vultures and octopuses and swindlers and bon vivants... *Merde*, as they say in France... And how about your activities? Are you right now sculpting the time, sculpting Time, giving it a first cry...?... Shall we meet in a winter grotto where the heat comes from an open fire... or on a beach... or on a mountain... where we can feel a smidgen of hope.

The process of life is a long story that must be changed, re-created, elevated. The true inspiration has a levitation power, as you know.

Tell me more about the hurricane you experienced! And your plans and dreams... The reefs are in danger, the deserts are increasing, the swindlers are everywhere... What shall we do?

Mangroves, large-scale shrimping, shrimp presidents, crazy man crazy... and all this talk about aliens coming...

24 and 25 December

You are going to the Bahamas, to the sun, the beaches, the dance, the easy-going life... A new adventure in your rich life full of people, processes, creative work... You write: "I made a model of a dancing-reclining-sitting-flowing body out of metal wire..." That's an important part of you, isn't it? – The dancing...

You asked me in your letter of 21 November 1996 about "the quiet side", to keep quiet during the "process of writing and composing". Do I keep quiet or do I talk too much? Well, I must say that the creative process is a mystery, even for myself. I might say a few words if somebody asks, but in Sweden people don't ask... Their days are full of TV, shows, business, entertainment, work, food, sleep... etcetera... Sometimes I speak without speaking; I fill the silence with a meaning I can only translate into poetry... And to be in the flow, to be in the creation, to be the creation is a gift you have. You must let go of the daily run of things and just be here and now, listening to the silence or the voice behind all voices, the tongue behind all tongues, the innermost being within yourself that knows why you are here...

Another question: "So, what do you think makes success in this life?" – To be honest, perhaps? True to your mission...?... But then of course you have to know what you are looking for and your part in a story bigger than your own life... T.S. Eliot writes in one of his poems:

58

"The soul of Man must quicken to creation." – Yes, we are builders... But what have we built? Is there a meaning or a plan or a God's voice... that we have not yet been able to understand? Man is skilful in his destructive habits. But is that his true nature? Have you read a little novel by Beckett called *The Lost Ones?*

To treat one's dreams seriously is, as far as I can see, to keep one's mind alive. Fate has always been doing me a lot of favours, and I listen to the voice of the Work... I read poets, Beckett, Joyce, Artaud, the Bible... yes, even the news, and the sky, of course; the faces of men, the trees, the flowers, the space that is full of sounds... And I'm learning to live from day to day, from time to time... hoping to meet you on my way through eternity...

I imagine you are happy now when you are in the sun on a beach. Or is there anything lacking? If you love you are loved and I believe that you love your life and the important part you play in this time of changes...

Watch out, anything can happen...

PS. Tell me your cherished dreams!

1997: Thailand letters, Malta,
the Inner Steppe...

The time is out of joint: – O cursed spite,
That ever I was born to set it right.

WILLIAM SHAKESPEARE

Now I can experience street scenes, dust... motorcycles, port girls exposing their feminine graces, TV series at the cafés, sleepers, hot air, elephants getting crazy in the jungle mountains in the heat, earthquakes of the body, full moon magic, fragrances from street temple flowers, golden temples, a distant Magnificent, and a turbulent motion in the awakening souls who have celebrated the vernal carnival here and everywhere on the Earth — waiting for a new revelation that is passing on the threshold of a solar AUM-time...

Yes, you probably know about the circulating prophecies, the comet Hale Bopp, the solar staging, all my initiation plays, the Ka breathing, the Kundalini exercises, the playful tantric way of life... transforming the dark history...

What are we doing? How do we behave?

A part of a letter from Chiangmai, Thailand.

Dear Shanti

11 January

Joyce writes: "Poor Isa sits a glooming so gleaming in the gloaming;" – And later on in *Finnegans Wake:* "Packen paper paineth whomto is sacred scriptured sign." – Always, never, ever... for ever... I am not, I am time, time is not... Have you heard of the global meditation on 23 January 1997? Will you join it? And what about the Hale-Bopp comet? And the new bluish-white star?

All this being... Sometimes I wonder if anybody can make sense of what is going on here and on other planets in the universe... It is night and I am trying to write, to use a typewriter that doesn't work very well... Perhaps I should use a pen?... I will try to go on in this night where everybody is asleep and now I am using a pen in the silent night full of snow and bewilderment. Europe is a stage, Canada... the world... You are doing some work in Canada. Is that your life task?

Passion, passionateness, passionless... Passive? No. I am a partaker, and I play... Namby-pamby? No. Proficient, of course... And soon (at the beginning of February) I have to move. Repairs will take place in the house where I live. – I don't know where I'll go. But I'll let you know...

Did you enjoy your stay in the Bahamas? – Or are you still planning to go?

1 February

In the nick of time, have some fun, be on the run, go for the sun, look for a road, be the goal...

Now reading Norman Mailer's novel *The Deer Park:* "Sweetie, you take a load off all my worries..." – Sadness, loneliness, drinks, clubs, bullfighters, call-girls...

63

Oh! Shakti, Oh! Shakti Maya, why haven't you come to save me from the ashes under the World Ash where I live? Askrikegatan means the Street of the Kingdom of Ashes or the Street of the Kingdom of the Ash (The World Ash, a tree in the old Nordic mythology). – Here I am. *Anima est Sol et Luna*, as you know...

I look for the Phoenix Park and not the Deer Park... *les cendres*...

Now sun morning glory, far calls, a machine world... and I don't belong to the Stockholm mucky-muckdom... The Doom is going on everywhere... "O, foetal sleep!" (Joyce)...

Where are you hiding? And to what purpose?

The desert, the snow, the sleet... And the trees, the strangers on the road in the wilderness... The snow-white mountains... The soul's solar power is strong... and what about Sky Man (the Man)?

Or Sun Man, the Solar Man?

I believe you know an awful lot of things, of secrets... and you are a living Soul Woman and a Solar Being, aren't you?... Basking in the sun of the Bahamas?

I have to move, but I don't know where... And the winter is cold and I am not a moneybags, but I have bags to carry and a lot of important work to do... In this strong morning-light I have a hope of solving my problems... And I know that the Universe is a labyrinth without beginning and without end and that a creation (a creative work) is going on everywhere... And you are there and I am here... We have to co-act and make it clear what we want...

Stop all the running crazy brains, give them peace... Let us shape a ring of people (the true hearts) and meditate in the morning sun outside some temple city in the desert, some future city or an ancient one... Just sit there in the rays of our sun, silent, breathing, filling our spirits with light words, light worlds...

The skin, the beach, the trees, the feet... Where do you walk, where do you talk? To whom, for what, in what manner?... Are you chatting up the crowd?

Krabi, Thailand, 20 February

On my way through time and in time I have landed in the tropics... I shall probably go back to Sweden in the middle of April.

Perhaps I shall find a "sand castle" somewhere by the sea – on some tropical island.

Lots of fruit, sea music, meditation... That's life! Isn't it? Do you agree? Too many Swedes in Stockholm are work and money addicts. I prefer the lazy life style of the true tropics, and it is a great relief to breathe the exile air by the sea.

25 February

At "The Last Café" on the Krabi beach... A bamboo table is my desk, the last rays of the Sun my musicians, the sound of the sea my background music...

I've lost my passport, I'm a universal being, my home is everywhere, what do I care... and I hope to see you somewhere on my way through the Milky Way...

On a train to Chiangmai, Thailand, 12 March

Gone through the purgation, the Bangkok hell,
I belong to no nation, have nothing to tell...
No home, no prison... Not eating pork,
nor chicken or Andaman shrimps...
I am an outcast but not a simp...

You will not find me at a brothel
or in a bar where one can be wretched or wrecked...
but perchance on a star where new thoughts are
    hatched...

The free of my hand to the spirit of Dawn,
and gone are the memories of all Bangkok prawns...

A change of body, soul, and mind
would be the next step I shall have to find...

Fed up with cheating, tricks, lash, mess and meeting...
tuk-tuk transport and infernal beating...

I have turned up at last
as a hermit of a shrine
beside the deepest river
of a forest divine...

The bedlam life all gone and forlorn.

But don't worry: There's no reason to cry.
I will soon be at home in the town of Chiangmai...

PS. From an art review in the *Bangkok Post* (12 March):
"At a time when Bangkok is in the throes of
environmental degradation and pollution, Yokota's
tranquil river scenes are a poignant reminder of a City of
Angels that used to be."

20 March

What about the pineal gland? Is it the same as the sixth
chakra? Is it alive? Does it produce the true miracles?
   A moment ago I met a beggar. She came with her
peasant hat, her blackened face, and her black Thai

trousers to my café table situated at a small lane in Chiangmai.

I'm staying in the centre of the city. Tropical laziness, reading fairy tales, joking, walking, visiting temples... And sometimes hill tribe villages.

The world is sleeping, the true word a dream, and the beggar a reality that belongs to the fairy kingdom where everything can happen.

The Night Bazaar, the Golden Fleece, the moon spirit, and the solar power... The bells of the temples, the temple drum on a mountain not far from Chiangmai... Ringing of bells, drum beats, the flower festivals... and there will soon be New Year celebrations all over this country...

"Side-street eating" doesn't interest me. I do eat noodles (without eggs), but not pork, meat-balls, fish-balls, etcetera. But I do like fresh fruit. Especially pineapple.

What are you doing?

And what about your creative work?

Europe could be a nightclub, a moon club, but it is not a nightmare...

I wish we could turn it into a solar stage! Or into a garden full of love-in-a-mists, love-birds, noble actors, and God men!

Is not God a man?

Virgin spring water, pure air, jungle sounds healing souls, light and a shadow play on the world stage...

Do you play?

Morning Glory
Blessings

PS. Write to my Swedish address. I'll probably be back in Stockholm at the end of April. And then: Lanzarote... But I'm not sure.

Hawaii is also a possibility – a good residence in this time of great changes.

The author at the temple of Wat Phra Keo in Bangkok.

A child in a hill tribe village, Northern Thailand.

Monks at the temple Wat Chedi Luang in Chiangmai.

PPS. In Chiangmai you can go to the temple Wat Chedi Luang and experience a chakra healing... Or you could sit close to a swimming pool swinging in the sun, swinging on the swing... reading about sun bears which have been saved from bear eaters who almost pay a fortune for a sun bear meal...

The best thing one can do is to go to a tranquil place in the jungle to see a waterfall and meditate in a jungle hut.

Now I have nearly forgotten the Bangkok inferno.

"Datta. Dayadhvam. Damyata.

Shantih shantih shantih"

(T.S. Eliot)

Semana Santa 1997

No to the work of the Inquisition and all power-seeking blockheads, detractors, and so on... *No* to the enslaving of people's creative power, *no* to the commercial stupidity ruling our modern towns and cities, *no* to the soulless manners prevailing among the so-called civilized peoples of the West, the East, the South, and the North... *No* to...

Now I can experience street scenes, dusk... motor-cycles, pert girls exposing their feminine graces, TV series at the cafés, sleepers, hot air, elephants getting crazy in the jungle mountains in the heat, earthquakes of the body, full moon magic, fragrances from sweet jungle flowers, golden temples, a distant Magnificat, and a turbulent motion in the awakening souls who have celebrated the vernal equinox here and everywhere on the Earth – waiting for a new revelation that is tarrying on the threshold of the solar AUM-time...

Yes, you probably know about all the circulating prophecies, the comet Hale-Bopp, the solar staging, all my initiation plays, the Ka breathing, the Kundalini exercises, the playful tantric way of life... transforming the dark history...

71

What are we doing? How do we behave?

Our creative ability is nothing to brag about if we consider all environmental facts.

In a pageant by T.S. Eliot the Rock (the Stranger) says: "Make perfect your will."

El Hallaj (an Arabic mystic) was sentenced to death in 932 after having declared: "I am God."

Christ, according to Saint John, once said (answering his opponents):

"Before Abraham was, I am."

Easter Week, Maundy Thursday

Heat, sun, sweat... I am watching wheels that once have belonged to a cart... But I am not living in a hovel. I am drinking tea and reading about Condwiramurs (*Conduire amour*) and am trying to figure out what *amour* is... Perhaps the medieval love initiation has something to teach us? Or are we too clever to understand?

Could you tell me the meaning of all this heedless destruction and all this killing and cheating...?...

Where do you find the *Logos*, the true Word, the true Work, the true thought, the true art, the true insight, the *gnose*, the Lazarus vision in a cooperative co-existence with the Logos...?...

In the *Bangkok Post* I saw that innocent people have been killed by Serbs (mercenaries) in Zaire – as a sadistic sport (maybe?), and I am aware that chemical fertilizers are spoiling the soil in Thailand and elsewhere... The petrol stench is a hell stench. I prefer a scent-laden garden, the Garden of Eden... to this Purgatory...

But there is hope. The *Bangkok Post* writes: "Doctors, psychologists and anti-smoking campaigners say they have had proof for years that smoking not only causes cancer and heart disease but is as addictive as heroin or cocaine."

I am not really a misanthrope, but I must confess: I cannot stand the haughty modern technical world and all its blinds...

In Frank Herbert's book *Dune* you can read: "A storm will come, our storm, and when it comes it will shake the universe."

There is a wind... And it is getting stronger... The sky is darkening... Thunder... The rain...

I am breathing the exile air, planning to go on with our solar revolution, being at home in all universes, trying to fulfil my true mission on Earth.

> *Best wishes*
> *from the*
> *thunder,*
> *the wind,*
> *and the*
> *Light*

The Golden Triangle Restaurant, Easter Day 1997

Sometimes it's no use speaking. Nobody will understand. It is better to keep quiet surrounded by narrow-minded New Age freaks and our ordinary fraud culture.

Death and the Maiden... A Shiva meditation. – I can hear the voice of the Stranger:

"Away with all nations, the evil spirits of the politics and the business, away with the roar of polluting engines, the falsifications, the megalomania of our concrete city civilization... and its noise..."

But sometimes you can hear the sterling starlings and happy frogs... Even in the midst of a city!

Chiangmai is such a city. Some central parts of it have got a real animated town atmosphere.

Yes, here I am, and a prisoner in a mad world, I am... And I can feel the iniquity of people's souls, the spurt, the spin... the win-win mentality...

73

Where are the silken girls, where are Martha and Mary...?...

Here? – Yes, at this very spot – at the Golden Triangle Restaurant where I can see two cart-wheels and remember my vagabond-drama – a jungle play where the Artist finally is Everybody on the River of Eternity.

Do you hear the cry – the howl before sunrise?!

Death... but no Maiden. Trials and crimes... but not enough consolation. And where is the once so famous generosity?

Now I recall the healing in a Buddhist temple, the good and evil spirits of the streets, the spirit gates, the spirit houses, and busy people buying sweets...

You can visit Pukhet, Savannakhet, Mae Sa Waterfall, Pang Thong Daeng (a village), Mae Sa Village and so forth...

The Snake Farm (near Chiangmai) is popular. Do we miss the Tempter of the Garden of Eden? Have we lost the true life energy?

"D'où es-tu?" – "From where are you?" – I point at the sun. But nobody understands...

In a newspaper I can read: "Soon Bangkok will erupt in flames..." – The Bangkok canals are sewers, food is contaminated... I hear thunder, flashes of lightning light up the cities... and especially Bangkok... The twentieth century soon gone, and how many have understood the deepest meaning of Mankind's story – the final History, the Resurrection?

> This world is a prison,
> but it might have a mission
> and on certain conditions
> I can see it as a vision,
>
> a forceful predilection
> for a world in connection

74

with the universal solar seed
helping us all to be freed
from the prominent grisly spell
that belongs to our famous hell...
- - -
my pineal gland, I must say,
works pretty well;
and I must confess:
I don't see all known creation
as a heap of mess...

Solar
and rain
and thunder
greetings

1 April

The impossibility of being here, the impossibility of
being, the sudden somersaults of life, the sodomy of our
celebrated culture, the big business, and the street sellers
carrying their yokes in the streets and the road-lanes (as
they call the small streets of Chiangmai)...

Some say: Beware of false and maudlin men and the
mausoleum (or museum) employees... And I agree.

Others say: Beware of newspapers, newsmongers, and
so on... Yes, I've given up all news at present and I'm
trying to tune into the song of the jungle frogs, the true
poets, the song-birds, the wise elephants...

Last night an elephant looked into a restaurant where I
was sitting. He (or *she*, to be correct) scrutinized the
eating people flapping her ears... while the elephant boy
was seeking to sell potatoes and cucumbers...

At the Top North Guest-House some guests were
staring at the sky looking for the comet Hale-Bopp...
that at least will be visible within a few days...

Yes, my dear Shanti, I must admit that I sometimes feel as if I were groping about in a dark and immense cave... where no light and no guide are to be seen... And somewhere outside this cave Mary and Martha are serving their guests...

Heat, stillness, roaring machines, the hot season... I am drinking hot tea, watching sleeping minds, remembering a dragon-fly I saw the other day close by a waterfall... And I will not forget the rafting experience, a bamboo raft on a river... I got soaking wet and was sprinkled all over with water... on a narrow raft on a narrow stream in the afternoon sun that was beaming through the leafy jungle of the banks...

Almost a baptism ceremony...

But I might still be in the cave while the world is a busy reality or riddle that I – for the time being – have not been able to grasp...

Bangkok, 6 April

Where are you?

I am sitting in my Bangkok apartment (12th floor, the Welcome Palace) eating cream crackers and drinking tomato juice. Outside: around forty degrees centigrade (above freezing-point). No chance to feel cold...

I have read in a newspaper that Toronto has had a quite cold April weather – colder than Stockholm.

I have been walking the big streets of Bangkok – an excruciating and almost killing experience, I must say... And sometimes I have looked upon the temples as shelters (or refuges)...

A lot has happened, is happening... Now I am moving. There is a smell of patchouli in the air, and I have moved to a café at Silom Village (an agreeable shopping centre in Bangkok). The heat is relaxing. Very few people here. Perhaps they have left the city and gone to the sea to enjoy the sea breeze... or are they sleeping? – The comet Hale-Bopp is passing somewhere up there... Unreal city. A waste land, and I don't know any madame who can read cards.

Prayers, praying, temples full of heavy incense smell. Krishna is popular, and Ganesha, Vishnu, Buddha, Shiva...

The Krishna priests have a lot to do. The blessing goes on, cymbals can be heard, songs...

And for the moment I'm drinking ginger tea (cold) at a table near a splashing fountain. On my table: a book about belated souls. I am thinking: the world is full of lost souls and sold souls... I am having a breather after having visited temples and spirit-houses, shops, and crowded pavements...

Spirit-houses (beautiful small shrines) can be found everywhere, and I've just seen a little mouse in such a house beside the Bangkok Bank – a huge palace in Silom Street (called *road*). The little mouse took care of the bank spirits, perhaps...?...

Hyacinth girls under the moon, temples, temples, and temples... and skyscrapers scraping the sky.

How much? Money, money, money... I offer you solar dollars, I pay in solar rays, I give you a solar mind palace... so you can forget all the suffering, the rubbish, the tin-roofs, the poverty... the stinking sewers, Bangkok's underground...

A peaceful mind, fruit everywhere, fruit for everybody ... is a dream I have right now...

> *I wish success*
> *to each and all!*

PS. *7 April 1997.* I would like to invite you to a "Maharajah Mystique" at a really attractive restaurant, the Maharajah's. – This nectar will (as they promise) "transport you right into the Hidden Gardens of the Moghul princesses". – But "Desert Winds" would be too strong for you. As they say: "The sands of Rajasthan are severe but with this delightful concoction of fruit flavours and tequila, the toughest warrior will relax".

Malta, 24 April

Thanks for your light letter to me in my role as a knight errant!

"Save the windmills for knights errant." – I've heard that these words were once written on a windmill on the island of Gran Canaria.

Yes, I sometimes look upon myself as a knight errant or as a knight lost in a dark cave of our time's wilderness. Are you the light bringer coming to my cave giving me new hope?

Right now I am sitting at the Café Marquée in Valetta (Malta) – in front of St John's Cathedral watching people in historical costumes and listening to medieval music.

I've not seen the famous Caravaggio painting, the "Beheading of St John the Baptist" (it has been removed to Florence for restoration). This painting inspired Samuel Beckett to his play *Not I* (a woman's mouth seen in darkness, a stream of words gushing forth). The Auditor in *Not I* is – as you know – a djellaba-clad figure.

The spring is here, the flowers, the birds... But Malta could be warmer. I miss the tropical heat of Thailand.

I've hurt my right foot (the great toe dashed against a stone), but never mind, I'll go on... in spite of the resistance and all the stones on the way...

Would you like to have "Knicker Bocker Glory: Ice cream served with fruit salad, nuts, panna, chocolate sauce and vermicelli"?

Wines & Spirits everywhere. But where is the high
spirit, the light spirit, the light lightness you mention in
your letter?

Music can be heard. The pageant is coming closer, the
knights of St John are on their way in the afternoon light.
The sun will soon vanish, and I read what you have
written: "Darkness feeds darkness." You also write:
"when you return to Sweden..." But I don't want to
return... and yet I know that I must go back to the old
battlefield to see if there is any chance to continue my
work in progress...

What about a meeting place in Europe? This summer I
might go to Scotland. I have to do some research work –
especially concerning the fate of the Saint Clair family
(the family of the Holy Light) and their role in the
spiritual history of Europe. I think I've told you that my
name is a heritage from that family.

But who knows...?...

The sun is setting. The music has ended. The people in
historical costumes have already passed, and I've finished
my cappuccino...

But now the music comes back. Stronger and stronger...
I can see a man carrying a red and white flag at the head
of the marching orchestra that stops near the steps to the
cathedral (St John's).

The bells toll. The air is chilly, the sleep goes on, the
money caves are dark, and you must work hard to be
able to pay the rent... No, I don't like to edge my way
along: nudging, hustling, bustling... is not my cup of tea. I
prefer a creative meditation on a river bank, in a rose
garden or on a mountain top...

The deserts of Africa are not far away, and the
powerful spring is here...

PS. I will soon take the ferry-boat (or the bus) back to my
tourist hotel (called the Petit Paradis) at Sliema.

To sit in a cavern (called "Happy Return"), to drink white wine and eat tomato soup and the next day stay at the Café Raphael, St Julian's, Malta, and read your words: "someone caressing the hair of a loved one" – that is, I believe, the beginning of a story worth reading.

Yes, you are right: the Buddhists practise a loving kindness meditation, and a lot of them are also aware of the black intoxication of our civilized world – as e.g. the monks of Wat Umong, a monastery on the outskirts of Chiangmai (Thailand).

"When you return to Sweden, perhaps you will see your neighbours... with new eyes." – That is another quotation from your recent letter.

I'd rather return to Eden instead of Sweden. What the neighbours want from me in Sweden is money. If I pay I shall be looked upon as a respectable citizen. If I don't... yes, you know.

The Master once said: "It is easier for a camel to squeeze through the eye of a needle than it is for a rich person to find the door to God's domain."

- - -

White horse, white solar light, huge Dome (at Mosta), calm sea, blue cave, dark caves, people strolling about in the sun...

Time for the timeless, the wordless, the silence... the unheard, unspoken words...

A cat is lapping milk on my table. *Shaman's Drum* (a periodical) can be seen close to the cat. My guest – the cat – is very polite. The same can be said about my other guest: an ordinary house-fly...

The sun is still strong. Sounds can be heard from the small harbour where the boats are green and red... and blue... A little well-dressed girl is approaching my table. She says: "The cat..."

The cat is purring in the sun, the sun is purring in the sky, the sky is purring in the space, the space is a blue bird in the Universe...

And I am a stranger (a knight errant) reading your words about love and kindness. Maybe you are right. The dark cave is perhaps not the whole story (history)...

What can we do?

Can our creative power bring about a paradise – at least a *petit paradis*?

PS. 27 April. The name of the hotel where I am staying is – as you remember – *Petit Paradis*.

PPS. 28 April. "Thou shalt love thy neighbour as thyself." So-called Christians usually quote these Christ words. But what kind of reality have they created? Pollution everywhere! – Sometimes one can hardly breathe. Even the Buddhists, the Muslims, etc. have joined our Western destruction club. – But I must admit: an awakening is taking place. Greenpeace people have for instance saved the last primeval forest in Sweden. What is happening in Canada? What about wind power, solar power, and other alternatives?

May

I pray and pray: Give us peace, generosity, creative blessings, space... Heaven must open, its riches pour down...

Fra Raphael Spinola, a member of a noble Genovese family, built a church and created a vineyard in order to be able to produce his own wine. He also constructed a market and boathouses for the fishermen where the Café Raphael and the San Giuliano Restaurant are now situated.

At the time of writing I am sitting at the Café Raphael, St Julian's, Malta. The sun has set, the green and blue boats are becoming black, the streetlighting is turned on, the lamps... The colours are gone, but the light-life is on, and the blue sky is darkening... The traffic, the street-noise, the busy life... are calmed down. And I ask: When do we start to build a solar time, a true heart-time, a holy world, feeling, dealing, acting... without all this hellish noise, pollution cars, haste, waste?... My lands set free at last, the human soul freed, filled with a dance, a feast, relieved from the heavy burdens of the past... Do you agree? Do you want to be freer than you are?

I pray and pray... and dream... and I am still here "in the last desert between the blue rocks" (Eliot), a slave and a prisoner in a waste land but not at my wits' end...

Stockholm – Gothenburg – Kiel – Eutin – Kiel... Now writing a sequel on a train between Eutin and Kiel remembering the magnolia flowers I just observed sitting on a lawn under a magnolia tree where I could hear spring birds while I was reading an article about Peruvian shamans healing busy civilized winter people...

Suddenly – in Eutin – the heat comes; a child says: "It's summer today." The flowers are on the trees, in the gardens... There is beauty before you, beauty behind you, beauty everywhere. It's incredible. Have I lived? with my sore feet and my vulnerable ego (self)? How much time have I wasted on Earth? on the line, off the track, on an elephant's back, at the castle of Plön (where a poet like Rilke could have stayed), at a lake of a forest paradise in some future mahamaya-ability existence?

The power of the mind has not yet revealed its true capacity for the creative human beings.

"From where are you?"

"From the Universe."

"No, I mean, which country?"

"The Universe, what else. Is that not enough for you?"

"But you must have a home country, a name, a birth date, etc."

... And off we go. Hallelujah! Take the hammer, put on the hair-raiser, repair your house, put on your shoes, be a nice boy, a nice girl... pay the rent, go to the bank, go shopping, beat down the price, but don't be everybody. That's too much.

I am glad you are helping distressed souls, helping them to find a new start, to be hopeful, and not of little faith... I suppose you have a lot of faith in yourself and in your work.

Once Buddha meditated under the Bodhi Tree and stopped the world wheel, the law of the old karma. Once Christ saw that the hearts of men must get out of the cave time, the dark Doom time. Once, beyond crucifixion and sacrifices, a new solar peace-time might be a possibility.

The sea is coming closer, a train, I can see, is white and red. The houses are silent, the street cars are prisons, the work goes on in the streets, in the harbour... At a station shop window in Kiel, I can read: "Küstennebel, Moskovskaya." A tramp says, "Grüss Gott". I feel quite alright, but what in reality is going on?

Are you there? out there in Space!? Hello! Tell me, where do we go, where do we end, why have we been here?

I can see the copper-blue sky, the copper-blue earth, the sea, white gulls, waves, and a blue star above the horizon...

We have to move up a little higher..."O Light Invisible, we glorify Thee!" (Eliot)... These words have stranded on my soul's coast while the sleep keeps on covering the souls, and my mind looks out for a new heaven and a new earth.

Take care!

Be of good cheer!

Samuel Beckett writes in his play *Cascando*: "Yes, correct, the month of May, the close of May. The long days. *Pause.* I open. *Pause.* I'm afraid to open. But I must open. So I open."

Sunday morning now. The wind, the sun, the hope that all holy souls will gather and start a glorious cooperation time. Stockholm is a stock-still city just now, a place where a few stockbrokers get richer and richer while the true creative people are trying to survive. Ecstasy, enthusiasm, joyfulness, pun mentality, and dance happiness are rare, too rare...

I don't care. But I have to pay the rent and all the bills, be somebody without anybody to talk to (all are too busy or have nothing to say). This is not a real world... But I can nevertheless speak to the trees and the sky and the sun. I am a tree man, a sky man, a solar man. I am. Here.

I might be able to stage some of my plays, and I am now looking for the right collaborators and the right stages. I am on my way... and can see some solutions...

If there is money, I might go to Scotland in July.

14 October

It is late, it is night; no stars can be seen. It is still green outside, and people are sleeping and perhaps dreaming of the twenty-first century. It's been a hard time, a time of trials, abuses, and a degradation of all mankind... The human mind is passing through an ordeal, and I should like to know why we can't realize that we all belong to an eternal play, a *maya-lila-play*... Or can you see another reality?

The play goes on, golden forests will soon shine in the sun, our Self-birthing is advancing, and the true kingdom

of man is here when we start to play, to dance, to sing...
to listen to the strange birds and the inner voices, the
sounds we have almost forgotten in a city world where
we can't buy a happiness we have lost and must find
again in our dreams...

My work to stage my play *Duel* has really been a duel in
a society full of men looking for entertainment – feeling
astray and lost and too busy... The theatre I had rented is
called The Peacock, a suitable name I think, and I don't
regret the outrageous adventure... After all: the last
performance was a great achievement and can be
conceived as a preparation for my whole-evening play
Day Dawns (not yet translated into English).

What about a pinkish beach villa on the island of
Tobago or on St Lucia?

Nothing is finishable. That's comforting.

A primitive life would suit me well...

Are you creating your new time?

What do you buy, what do you dream, what do you say
to your friends at night by a fire? Or in a castle, or by the
sea?

Do you talk about our present reality: the wind, the
nuclear doom, the earth changes, the spirit gates, the split
of the minds, the demons ruling weak souls, the abusive
talk you can sometimes hear, the foul smell from the
garbage chutes, our inability to create peace, to listen to
the inner voice, to be like a living fire forever...?...

To eat grapes on a sunny hill by the sea – wouldn't
that be the right thing to do, eat grapes, drink some
good wine (ecological cultivation), greet the light, meet
the wind, dance on a hill and forget the disasters of the
cities...?...

I hope I can leave Sweden in November. But I am not
sure. I feel the need of a living atmosphere, a solar time
life where every breath is a poem.

I recently saw a film-version of Shakespeare's *Hamlet* and remember the words: "The time is out of joint: – O cursed spite / That ever I was born to set it right!" – Yes, what is this life? A wind-swept desert or a sultry cellar? Haply we believe in our poor discourses of reason, our poor imagination that is not even able to see a flickering light in our immense cave. Not to mention the slings and arrows of our daily talk – and to what purpose?

You whom I have seen in other corners of this universe – what are your longing, your soul's true garment?

I am lost, indeed, and the desert is vast... The wind of your soul is sacred music to my ears. I am alone on an eternal strand; cities and a dearth of money – spectres of the past. What shall I extol? Life's green meadows or walled prisons where butterflies and flashes of merriment are but distant spectres...?...

Conflagrations in Asia, pollutions, and mafiosos everywhere. Can we now gather all the solar minds and start a new Era's day? We hope for the best. What have you to suggest?

Have you read "master Shakespere"? He is a riddle, as you know. Nobody knows exactly who he was.

"To be, or not to be..."

All this mortal coil... What shall we do? Evil spirits everywhere. Demons ruling the world. Especially Stockholm. But I don't know. Mad spirits are governing people's minds: attacks and fires and hells and total confusion... and clumsy manners and dark souls... in all cities, of course... What shall we do?

"For who would bear the whips and scorns of time:"?

Enough of contumely, of insolence, of shocks, and mad assaults... Yes, we need spirit-houses at every corner and men with noble demeanour in this autumn darkness...

The winter is approaching, the coldness, the storms...

From season to season, from oasis to oasis, from promise to... No. A wind. I can hear it. A holy desert. I can feel it. A mind, a body, senses, feeling... And a voice, a purification, a meeting...

This life is not life.

But it could be. Not words, words, words... But a solar word, a solar world. Can you create it? Can you give birth to a blessed world? Now!?

PS. Bills, bills, bills... and the survival of the fattest. But I don't know in this end-Time labyrinth where some people think they can channel what is going to happen... Who are the real losers?

Are dark wizards ruling the world or are the rulers simply stupid? A few are getting richer and richer and the poor are everywhere. There are a lot of beggars (mostly young) in Stockholm, the cultural capital of Europe next year. Robert Lepage is invited, of course, and I might be able to do something... I have sent in applications. But do they want a solar revolutionary?

And where is the wisdom?

Bill Gates lost a lot of money (billions poorer in one night). That's what people are talking about. The Stock Exchange, the market, laundered money, and the Nobel Prize for literature to Dario Fo. I like him, but has he written something you just can't miss?

We really need some bewitching light power in this autumn darkness. How on earth is mankind going to survive?

Autumn life is not my life. I mentioned the autumn darkness in my previous letter. What is life in its deepest sense? A yawning drone? No. Endeavour and endeavour and... Talks and drinks... and bars and musicals where the devil, the black rider, tries to control everything. More money, more "love", more depressions...

I wish I could turn all this mad world upside-down.

Do you know some noble human beings, some real free spirits?

These words are my vehicles in a world I am trying to grasp before it is too late. Silence. Night. The sleep is going on... and I know that a little change can release the breath. Sometimes it is suffocating. Why do people build prisons everywhere? And tell me: Is there any living creed that speaks the truth?

I am trying to communicate. But do I succeed? Where are all the new-world-builders gone? Tell me! Can you? I am steering my soul ship on an infinite sea. Is there an island somewhere, a coast, a dawn, a sunrise... and a soul meeting?

Do you see the colours of Dawn in this night? And what am I supposed to do? Release the prisoners? Open the gates to a new earth and a new heaven or haven?

Tell me, you who know how to sing a tune that can bring peace to my mind, tell me the truth...

23 November

Do you think that the *International Herald Tribune* will herald a new Era's Day? – "Events that were unforeseen a short while ago are now driving political and financial decisions that are re-shaping our world." – That's what they say, the IHT-people. Are you interested in up-to-date stock closings? No, I don't think you are. But I suppose you read information on art, entertainment, fashion or food.

We are shaping and re-shaping – but who are the real makers of the world?

It's overcast, dull, gloomy... No day, at all. But I do believe I exist. Perhaps in a world without time or beyond time? Time is a liar. Eternity speaks the truth. Or can you find a reliable truth in momentous times? – Sometimes I believe I am a stranger coming from a yet unknown future *mahamayability* (a Joyce-word?), and now I am *ticking up on time* (again Joyce) trying to find out what all this means: the flights and the beaches, the moon and the sun kisses, the meditation at the foot of an Indian fig-tree, my time in Chiang Mai (Chiangmai), the mist, the absent women, the earth, the water, the sea, the talk...

The desert is full of spirits, the cities are full of bodies, singing voices are doing their best to convince me that life will never end, and I am not reading all the newspaper articles that give you a view on the fornication business that is going on everywhere.

The palms, the dreams, the sun, the prices... and our wicked generation and the next... No, let us talk about something else, let us have a look at your paintings, your or my red skies and black earth, our breathing bodies in an air that is polluted and full of thoughts and desire; the legs, the steps, the fingernails, the fingertips in a sunny air where we can feel the heat and a message we can't translate...

Yes, it's hard to land on earth, to be here... to beat time. But it is possible, as you know and can remember. I don't have to read the *Washington Post* to understand who you are. And now I ask: *Where is our next rendezvous?* – On this overcrowded earth there are a lot of empty places where we can find a room for our poetic creativity, the blue and the red mood, the dream conversation...

Thanks for calling! Now waiting for your message.

PS. "Till daybowbreak and showshadows flee. Thus be hek. Verily! Verily! Time, place!" (*Finnegans Wake*)

27 November

I am here. Where are you? Come closer, I can't hear you, I can't see you, it's terribly dark in here, all lights are gone, the snow is wet outside, the streets are full of shadows, a street car named Desire has gone astray, you can hardly sleep, the day is dark, the night is darker, the people want more money, and of course: more and more entertainment, and so forth...

Wipe out the past, be here in the present... The past night is full of mistakes, errors, and crimes. Even brave and learned men have behaved like lunatics. Will the Mars mankind be better than humanity on Earth? I am not sure. And what will happen with all the emotions and the sensuality? Will the emotional man have time and possibility to develop? Now he is almost blind, and wise teachers are lacking. Or do you have another opinion?

I really hope you will have time to answer all my questions in the letters you've got this year. In your stream of consciousness you have all the answers. Even your silence is an answer.

When I shut my eyes I can hear a storm across the steppe, I can see a runaway horse and a woman who is laughing, dancing and laughing in the storm. The clouds are red, a song can be heard, the woman's song, and the weather is calming down... It's soon the right time for everybody, and I believe I shall have a possibility to go on existing... Maybe somebody (a living soul) will speak to me some day – on a mountain, on the steppe, in the wind...

90

"Hello, who are you?"

"I am nobody – a no-body, a soul-body trained to the habit of hearing: no, no, no..."

"But hasn't the red sky said: Yes, you are welcome, your work is needed, your fellow workers are increasing in number..."

"But I cannot hear what they are saying. They are too far away, and the only thing that is in my mind is a woman's song on the steppe..."

> *Solar*
>> *song*
>>> *greetings*

PS. I do believe in a light future. Some day I shall find it. Some day it will be my home. – What do you think, what do you sing?

29 November

In one of my letters (Oct. – 97) I said something about wine. I very seldom go out wining and dining. I prefer the whine of the wind, and if I listen to my inner sounds I can hear the whining wind on the steppe and a song... but no words. The wind is too strong. A woman is singing under clouds torn to pieces by the wind...

I wish I could hear the words and see who it is. She must have something to say. Perhaps she will give me worlds and words I have forgotten, worlds I have lost, scents I have never felt...

It is late. The world watch has stopped. Is somebody here? Somebody I can't see?

It is night. No moon. The city is almost silent. Dream time? Yes. And the body is tired. Somewhat. But not the spirit. The straw, the stream, the strand, the stray...

I can see a cactus, a couple of palms, typing paper on the floor, lamps and bookcases. The sandman is approaching, the dream rivers are coming closer, the dream banks, the sea, the desert, the steppe and the woman. Her voice is far off, but it will come closer. I have a presentiment of a wonder of wonders. We have not been waiting in vain. Time is here.

16 December

Thanks for your letter and art card of 4 December. I get your point. You wrote: "I think we need to find the warm place, the place of simplicity and order, to find ourselves well situated in that which surrounds us and then the spirit has a real place to land, to move forward, to carry us."

In a way I am a nomad, lost in a city where people are too busy. But I can of course enjoy wonderful food if I can afford it.

The other day I saw a movie called *The English Patient*. Have you seen it? Did you weep? Did you feel at home in the desert landscape?

When I shut my eyes the song can still be heard, the steppe song and the desert song. I remember the solar sights and the moonlight, the deserted streets... and women huddled up in a barn, in a cornfield, in a howling storm... far away from the dead cities where suffocated souls yell and scold... Or what is going on at this very moment?

You ask: "Who can you love in your life?" – My answer is: A child for instance – a creature open to all these incredible miracles going on everywhere. And I do love the song that fills all the space, the steppe light, the desert night, your laughing mood under the red moon (a long time ago), your letters and your light temper in this winter time.

I saw a glimpse of the sun (a companion I love) a month ago. We are greatly in need of high spirits in this time of darkness. And I am glad that you enjoy your life.

The world is a formulation in progress. Our daily responsibility cannot be overlooked.

Nations and damnation?... No. Clarity of vision is what we need.

Can you imagine a solar power world (a truly creative world) ruled by wisdom, compassion, peace... and a free spirit?

Isn't there in every soul a laughing eternity body?

Bless the World and you are blessed.
Bless the Word and you are blessed.
Bless the Sun and you are blessed
By the Sun, the Word and the World.

1998: From India and from the Cultural Capital of Europe

In that earopean end meets Ind.

JAMES JOYCE

*The Virgin-Maiden in a sculpture group in
a church in the Old Town of Stockholm.*

Dear Shanti

The impossibility of being here, the impossibility of being somebody in a world full of bodies... Now it is 1998 and the cultural capital of Europe, Stockholm, will be inaugurated. The fogs prevail. It is a misty world. The Virgin-Maiden is waiting...

I've lived a country life in the mist for some days. On New Year's Eve I was in a villa in a forest many Swedish miles from Stockholm together with cowmen and dairymaids – drunk cowmen pawing... about and silent dairymaids in a sofa. Wood flames in the fireplace, but I don't want to perish in the flames. And I cannot stand clumsy drunk people who do not even talk about the earth spirits. But I know of course: the forlornness is great everywhere – not only in a misty forest where cowmen work and eat their meat dreaming of a paradise they lost in their childhood. They hunt, they drive, they work hard and dream of love in a dark and cold and drab winter...

It is raining, almost spring climate. Victoria Chaplin is dancing in the air at the Orion Theatre (Stockholm), where I took part in a winter solstice ceremony on 21 December 1997. I read texts in Swedish and in English – my words about a still unheard world... I am on a world stage with my willpower and my dreams and wishes... It is high time. The storm lurks around the corner. The greatest possible adventure – life – is going on... And we must turn the Boat of Millions of Years (the seat of peace)... and sail backwards through infinity until our earth bodies are nothing but fairy tales in the non-history of eternity...

No stench any more from cowsheds and stupid engines. The wheel of the great world cycle is turning. *Ho hang!*

Hang ho! The money too is gone. No worries when our minds start to whirl in the whirlpool of our true cosmic reality... No false relations, relatives, feelings, hurts, blames... I can assure you that the worst tormentors (the blind demons) will find no tools and no victims when all ages have had their last say and the new World Word is arising... Yes, forget about the borders and the shadows in the doors, the lack of souls, living souls, Word people, poetic minds, time strangers... The real Strangers have entered at last, and the whole stage will be reshaped... Soon the fall will end and the rise start...

Now in this studio in the universe it is silent. The books, the lamps, everything... Is anybody there?! – No answer.

I don't know where you are. In the Californian sun, I guess, having some fun, moving about in the wind by the sea or in the snow on a mountain... Or are you looking out of a window with somebody you know and always will know...?

Yes, I remember your Christmas card showing a woman and a girl who could have been you and your daughter in another life... Or perhaps in this one?

12 January

Back through time, all ages gone, the false world a heap of ashes... See, be, turn backwards, let all your old thoughts burn down, become ashes... Be the impossible future of the past, the first ray after this long night full of ugly demons. Speed up "the grand fooneral" (Joyce), rejoice... You don't have to speak to dead walls any more, no evil spirit can hurt you, no poor blockhead can be in your way. "The golden wending" (again Joyce) is coming closer... Listen! – A dream tongue is speaking.

Backwards through time. No ending, of course. "Tiers, tiers and tiers. Rounds." The Wake is here. Finn again.

98

Wake up from sleep. Yes, I suppose you know about "the eversower of the seeds of light" and the cold old souls "in the domnatory of Defmut".

Why should I listen to reason – the reason of the dead or sleeping souls? Their reason makes me sick at heart. Must we invent a new tongue because no tongue can speak the truth any more? And I am not a bore. I don't keep silent when I see the imprisoned souls lost in "the domnatory of Defmut".

Do you know the prophecies of e.g. the Kabbala? Or what the Hopi elders say about this time? I've just seen some television programmes dealing with prophets, prophetesses, predictions, and the like. But I am not convinced.

The Creation is a work in progress. Great poets are re-creating our world and the minds of people... Or am I wrong? Has anybody listened? Is not nature a good listener, the birds, the sea, the wind, the fire... a woman in a hut on a mountain in a snowstorm at night? Yes, she hears the tale of tales: the music behind the new soul-words born at this very moment in the heart of Mankind, and the poet is there and finds the true expression, the true formulations...

Past now pulls. Forget, remember... Be the Song, your song, dance the Dance, your dance... Is this the last chapter of my first Shanti book? Maybe?

Drip, drip, drip... drop... drops... The inauguration of Stockholm as the cultural capital of Europe will soon take place. I am not invited. I'm probably blacklisted. Never mind. The new mind is here, the new world mind.

Hopefully I shall go to India, and there somewhere I might find a good printing house that can print one of my books. Don't you think Indian readers will understand and appreciate what I have written? And what about you? – Do you still sing Indian songs? Can you hear the music of the intergalactic musicians?

Full moon today. Not cold at all. I have just experienced a Rite of Ascension and feel relaxed. After a meditation rite you start to listen. The song is still there – far away on the steppe.

The impossibility of being, the impossibility of being in love, the impossibility of feeling the presence of some-body I've always known, the strength, the clearness, the utmost subtlety, and tactfulness...

It is rather cold now, and I don't know where the smile that lives is hiding – in which room, in which city, in which country?

I know we have met: a glimpse of life has ignited the fire on this enormous churchyard or sleeping stage. Why didn't I open my mouth and speak when I could have spoken? Now the only thing I can see is the waste land. No, that is not the truth... I've perhaps reached a border, the cold wind is strong, it's dark around me, voices are echoing in a tunnel and you are approaching... I can feel your presence in your absence, and what should I do?

Should I listen to some music – *Amando e desiando* by Benedetto Gareth? – Or should I consult a seeress?

Something is shaking my heart – a vibration I have never known before... I'm waiting, but the stage is empty, the forests are very dark, the sea immense, the fever of life is beating everywhere, and soon the flames of hope will come... The fire, the ice, the city, the winter, the soul, the body, the silence...

Yes, yes, yes... speak, raise the cups, be here, let me have another chance, to breathe, to see, to dance, to fill all the air with sweet fragrance so that the land can bloom again, so that the eyes can shine again... What we can imagine today may be a reality some day...

6 February

Are you on the throne? Am I? Was I ever in a body?
A body, I was.

Here I am – in a snowy and cold land. The land of my dreams is far away. I remember words from Samuel Beckett's play *Embers:* "Bitter cold, white world, not a sound"... What shall I do? Listen to a Russian-orthodox choir that will soon be singing in a church in Stockholm? Yes, that's an idea.

Cold feet, cold arms, silent trees... Silent newspapers, silent theatres, silent souls... And you are silent. Everybody is silent. But I am not... No engines around at this very moment.

How do you put life into a stage where everybody is asleep?

People have said: You are ahead of your time. But what is time? Do I belong to this time? Do you?

It's dark, almost night. A breathing is going on, no moon, no stars... Silence. People have locked their doors, they are sitting in their sofas, waiting... What is going on? Have you heard the news? Are we still alive... and what next?

India is a distant dream. All this long time in this Ash Kingdom, in this asphalt world... But there is life, I am sure. People (some) are singing in the Underground, and a few are praying in the churches while the waiting goes on. A girl told me yesterday that she was from the Pleiades. Yes, why not! From where are you? Lady of silences, where have you been, where do you go, what are your plans, your hope, your dreams?

101

You are not here. I believe I am. Maybe I ought to see Shanti Vana or Shakti Sthal. It is spring. Birds are singing in the guesthouse garden. The sun is bright. The sky is clear.

I gave a beggar 2 rupies this morning. Not much, I agree. But the beggars are many... Too many. She (the beggar) looked old and infirm. She carried a stick and could not pull herself up. I told her to lift up her head and look at the sky. Even a beggar woman in rags belongs to the sky.

But what shall I say to all the speed-intoxicated petrol-car-drivers spoiling the air, filling this city (and all cities) with infernal noises. A traffic jam in Delhi is a total inferno – that not even the poet Dante could have predicted or imagined.

Speed, stench, rush, poverty, cruelty, ignorance, insensibility... What shall we do?

In an article (a press cutting) I've read that a Turkish muslim called Turki killed my friend Hans Christian – an atrocious deed that you know about. He (the killer) prayed to Allah (according to the newspaper article) and Allah (who is he?) told him to do what he did.

A commemorative performance and programme (including speeches) will soon take place in New Delhi. Organizers: the Himalayan Research and Cultural Foundation. I will give a speech on that occasion.

I am now longing for the silence, the desert, the mountains, the blue rivers, the animated dances, the drumbeats in the jungle, the silver moon above a hill top, the blue and wise spirit soaring in the clean air in a Virgin country...

Time is running out, the old time, and a new breath of a new Era's day is coming closer... Who are in this time holding the world's destiny in their hands?

Dirt roads, bent bodies, camels as silhouettes towards a
darkening sky, an evening horizon... yes, earth is a rich
spot in the universe.

Is there a better home?

> *Indian moon*
> *and solar*
> *wishes*

16 March

Fever, fever, fever... I'm very weak, but the sun is strong
here in Jaipur, the capital of Rajasthan. I'm eating fresh
fruit (bananas, oranges, papaya...) and drinking fruit
juices... My life has not come to an end. I cannot leave the
stage right now. There is still a lot to be done. Is there –
on the whole – a limit, an end? – I'm doubtful. – The
universe has no limits and no real end, so why should I
end my life in a city close to a desert?

Starving children, beggars of all ages on the pavements
where you can also meet cows, dogs... and both curious
and very kind (smiling) people.

Pink walls, pink palaces, wise elephants... and too many
stinking and noisy vehicles... But you can take a bicycle-
riksha and not an auto-riksha... Once some people used
to go by air – in *vimanas* – that you can read about in
ancient folk-tales.

(This letter is not completed.)

Jaipur, Rajasthan, 30 March

Fever has ruled my body at least two weeks. I feel better
now... the coughing, sweating, and so on, belong to the
past.

"India's three foremost problems are", said a Jaipur student the other day, "people, poverty, pollution". – In the ancient folk-tales of this country you can read about *vimanas* – swift planes that maybe didn't pollute the air as much as our modern technology.

Black clouds over Himavant? – Possibly! – Here the sky is clear, and the midday sun is very strong. I dream in my little "solar temple" – a beautiful room that belongs to a palace-like building (the Umaid Bhawan). Pink walls and barriers (rails, banisters), Oriental vaults, a pleasant garden... I'm sitting on my balcony, relaxing and recovering strength, after a time of trials and fever.

The regeneration time has come.

Now I would like to cradle in a cradle in a garden full of morning glory. No doomsday horror any more, no simple-tons around... Just light, silent light, and whispering distant voices... A song? Yes, singing voices that – in a way you don't understand – open a new gate to a lost paradise.

Hotel Pushkar Palace, Rajasthan, India. Easter 1998

Silent afternoon, I feel sick. Wrong food. And now I must cure myself. – It is *Domingo de Ramos* today, and also Rama's birthday. I suppose you have read the famous Indian epic *Ramayana*.

Pushkar, where I've been a few days, is a rather quiet, holy town with a lot of temples – e.g. a special Brahma temple known by pilgrims all over India.

Sunny afternoon at the Pushkar Palace (a rather expensive hotel): I can see the holy Pushkar lake in front of me.

Holy *ghats* (steps leading to the lake), holy cows, pigs, goats, parrots... and beggars. Yes, at least some of the beggars (one of them has no legs) seem to be holy. – Fortune-tellers, astrologers, brahmins... Who is not holy?

At the hotel Umaid Bhawan, Jaipur, India.

Facing the altar of the Brahma Temple, Pushkar, India, and musicians close to the holy Pushkar lake.

Aham Brahmasmi (I am Brahman).

– From where are you? – From which country? – How old are you, etc.? – Yes, you know: all these questions. – Sometimes I point towards the sky. I say: *The Sun.* But mostly I tell them about *Waveland* – a newly founded Greenpeace-country whose borders (or: only borders) are the ones that Nature and Imagination are creating in your mind.

In a way I can call myself a Greenpeace rainbow warrior or a knight errant in a world where I can hardly understand all the actions and reactions filling all media.

I remember the initiation the other day by the holy Pushkar lake... A young Brahmin acted as an initiator. – He made me repeat all he said (God-names, mantras, good wishes, etc.). I sacrificed flowers, spreading their petals on the lake where people had a dip with their clothes on.

The Initiator said: "Now your old karma is gone." – I showed him some breathing exercises, looked into the afternoon sun, got some holy lake water in my right hand. Water on the head, on the forehead, on the crown...

I believe you would like the songs in the temples and the music and songs by the desert people using flutes, drums, and some kind of fiddle. Here you find the spirit of a living soul.

Have you ever been really present on the Earth? Have I? I am not sure. – People from the country use "Ram-Ram" as greeting words. They have more earth-and-sky-knowledge than city people in general.

Two nights ago: a strange phenomenon. I noticed after arrival at this little oasis town two desert hills (bust-like) rather close to each other. I recognized one of my paintings inspired by a dream I had about ten years ago. – Now the only missing thing, I thought, is the heavenly spectacle in that very special dream I had. – Believe me or not: It came while I was sitting at a rooftop restaurant. A storm came, rain, lightning... I watched the two hills of

107

my dream and my painting, saw the dramatic light play
around and between the hills... after sunset.

It was – as you might have said – outrageous. And you
could read a message – a time message.

Stomach-ache, hot air, a life I'm trying to understand.

Is this day a day of penance? Who and what shall we
glorify?

In a paper you can read that the super-rich of today
are work addicts. And what about you? – Have you time
to breathe, relax, dream, imagine, create...?...

> *Holy Week greetings*
> *from Pushkar's holy lake*
> *and temples*

Har(i)dwar, Maundy Thursday 1998

The lightning over *Ganga*,
the mist, the thunder
and the Purification.

My old mind is gone
at Haridwar, God's Gate.
Red, pink, light-blue houses,
red temples at the foothills
of Himava(n)t*...

DA
The thunder spoke,

and my time, a river-boat,
turned towards the source,
the Re-birth... the Solar Birth...

---

*Himalaya (Himavat). In T.S. Eliot's poem *The Waste Land*:
Himavant. *Ganga* is the River Ganges.

The red and yellow flowers
shone in the dark shade...

And the Sun said:
Om Shantih, Shantih, Shantih.

Yes, I have survived. I have saved my skin and can now
meet the new spring in Europe...

What do I remember? Well, Ganga, of course, the
procession during the *Khumbh Mela,* holy people
(sadhus, etc.) with their resplendent dresses, the peaceful
cows, the night-scented flowers of the tobacco plant, the
birds chirping before sunrise, the mosquitos...

and the Resurrection...

I admired a peacock's train, I bought a peacock fan and
gave it to a naked beggar child in a busy street in Delhi,
and I'll never forget his happiness after having received
this fan.

Who am I now after having thrown away my old karma
and having purified myself in the whirls of Ganga? Do I
need a baptizer? No, I don't think so. I have risen from
the ashes, I have started to listen... and can hear music,
a whisper, a wind, a choir-singing in a primeval forest
where the spirits are full of grace...

*With India still in my memory I wrote down this Time
Message:*

The Masters are here: this is the Master time outside
time. All ages are gone, and I don't want them back. The
heat in the afternoon... The old memory... Pain and
trials... No, I don't want it back. Heat, silence, and noise...

I cannot forget the silence in the Lotus Temple (New Delhi), the large silent temple hall without idols, a free spirit in the air, the breath and a silent prayer... Has it finally come: the Resurrection Time?

To greet the sun at sunrise on Easter Sunday is – in a way – a Second Coming.

A new fire lit. And I don't feel the loss of the old karma. Ganga has purified and regenerated me, and the stories of the past (degradation, poverty, mockery, and so forth) is something I will never want back.

The peacock's train... an excellent campus restaurant, and mosquitoes attacking...

Once I had no space, no time, no room. But time has now come for me to fill my space, my time, my room... And the wedding guests are waiting to be called...

In a spring-tree a bird sang to me:

"She is here, she has finally come to inaugurate a New Era's Birthday, a New Solar Era's Bride and Bridegroom Day!"

18 July

Have you read *The Subterraneans* by Jack Kerouac? – a book where young people (hoboes, etc.) get high on tea and benny. Not ordinary tea of course... Hip, cool, unattainable Heavenly Lane hipsters... in San Francisco, a city you know, I imagine...

Summer, July, Stockholm, dark skies, quiet, not even a bird can be heard. This is the cultural capital of Europe. They are doing their best, I suppose. I mean: the cultural people. Not always: corruption, disintegration, entropy... You know: all these academic and scientific half-lights or lies... Everything is dying, I know, but that is not the whole truth. Why are people so afraid of the living, the living truth, the living man, the ongoing creation of the boundless universes we inherit and create in all our lives!?

I can hear voices behind curtains and in cellars, dreamers using infernal combustion engines, a stupid and diabolic technology. Explosion instead of implosion. Petrol instead of air and water. Etcetera. The inventor Nikola Tesla was on the right track, and he knew how to use and master a free, liberating and uplifting energy technology... And I know there are Tesla followers living in Canada.

Here Greenpeace people are aware of the so-called greenhouse effect. We must change-over to renewable energies. That's the only solution.

It is as if the earth had ceased to move. Not a word is heard. Not a wind, hardly a breath... the trees don't move. They are silent. Even the flowers, the harebells, the roses, the pot marigolds... It is not yet 1999, not yet 2000...

I believe now that this universe is a good-enough-stage for you and me and all the other actors playing my plays and other plays. A beggar in the dust can also be a sun. Yes, I know: I remember a beggar I met at Pushkar in India. In Pushkar I felt the living pulse, albeit I was hardly living... And there by the holy lake I left my old karma. I threw it away...

What will now happen? How shall I act?

Shall I go to West Samoa and wait for the year 2000 to open its gate...?...

No, not yet at least... And what will you do on this immense stage? Dance and celebrate? Listen to Patti Smith singing "Godspeed", "High on Rebellion", etc.?... And drum and sing and find out the secrets behind cosmic and earthly waves...?...

The true heart of the world might be hidden somewhere on an almost inaccessible iceberg. Who will find it and give it back to humanity?

PS. 19 July. Dead or alive? Sometimes I don't know. I read Joyce's *Finnegans Wake:* "A hundred cares, a tithe of troubles and is there one who understands me?" – Animals are also people. Selma Lagerlöf knew that, possibly. Have you read her books? – Now the sky is clear. The performance is over. The theatre tent is empty. The dream lives on.

Waveland, 29 July

The bumblebees are among my best friends. They keep me company on my balcony in the sun. They are visiting my flower boxes where wild clover is blooming.

Who are you? From where are you?

Sometimes I don't know what to say. Just now I'm trying to listen to the voice of the innermost soul of the universe. Is there a forgotten message hiding somewhere? What is fate or destiny? Is there a plan, a personal fate? Is there something behind this curtain of illusions? Titles, careers, money... Yes, a lot of people believe they are something, but they can't even understand a birch, a fir, an oak or a bumblebee...

Once a man in Dalecarlia (a Swedish province) greeted me with a smile and the words: "Welcome to Sweden!" – I must say I felt honoured. But it was a long time ago. Sweden is now in many ways a past history. Waveland, Europe, and the Universe are more suitable places of residence.

I'm writing this letter watching the bumblebees. They are always busy collecting nectar and pollen. They don't make war, they don't attack... They don't misuse the words. They are humming, sucking, and flying from flower to flower... They have their homes in the earth and can't understand why we build such ugly cities.

Do you have a garden? Are you a gardener?

What kind of fairy tales are you reading? what kind of
fairy tale are you creating – a tale about a blue bird and
a princess imprisoned in a tower?

The sky is clear. Men are fighting and working and
sleeping. But there are also people who dance and forget
about all prejudices.

The other day I listened (at a theatre) to the theatre
and film director Robert Lepage. He is directing a play in
Stockholm and was interviewed by a dramatic critic.
Robert was of course aware of the importance of playing
and not just acting. In his stagings words are not so
important. *Tittle-tattle*, yes, anything would do... But
what happens if you can say anything and mean nothing?

Well, I can see that he is a very gifted multimedia man
and he knows how to tell stories, but is that all?

Do you create your own life's history, your own life-
work? Are you freer than a bumblebee, than an old oak,
than a sun in the universe? And where have all the
colours come from?

White, pink, blue... The scent of jasmine, roses...
fragrances in a virgin forest, on a virgin mountain, by the
sea, in a jungle, etcetera...?...

People need flowers. Do flowers need people or just
bumblebees?

> *Light*
> *summer*
> *wishes*

Waveland, 12 August

Thanks for your letter where you advice me to anchor
my heart... on this wild sea... Have you seen Bruegel's
painting *Storm at Sea* or his *The Magpie on the
Gallows*? The menacing gallows is there while the dance
goes on and people laugh and love in the sun.

113

Jack Kerouac (who was on the Path) says in his book *Some of the Dharma*: "Buddha never said that this evil world would never end."

In your last letter you state that you are "an ambitious woman in the world" and you are adding: "and want to make my mark so to speak". – Very well, I can understand. But I must also confess that at times I've hoped to be able not to leave any mark at all. To be a man of mark – what is that? Anyhow I don't belong to our famous black market, and now I should like to shake the dust off my feet and disappear somewhere – maybe to a hut in a desert.

According to your letter you intend to go to India in the year 2000. Yes, why not! – And if you go to the little town of Pushkar in Rajasthan maybe you will meet the beggar who has no legs – the one I told you about in a previous letter. I shall never forget his shining smile. I used to call him the Sun of the Dust. Almost every day during my stay in Pushkar I was passing him, and I can remember how he looked up from his dusty earth place in the sun as if he wanted to say: The heart of the world is here in the dust, in the sun, in the heat, in this suffering that can be changed into a great joy when the two worlds meet...

Yes, somehow or other he really understood... And I can also remember the desert troubadours and their songs, their natural, effortless way of singing.

Millions of years are now passing by while I'm writing these words, looking for a possibility to print a book I think you would like, dreaming fairy tale dreams and creating a ladder that can reach up to a new earth and a new heaven... A woman stands at the utmost end of a dark lane. Who is she? Is she waiting for me to join her?

I've just finished an essay on Beckett and his interest in painting and painters' works.

Who is there?

A breakdown in the transmission. I can't hear you.

114

"No," I shout, "I don't believe in entropy. That's not my religion."

Two thousand years. Nine... I don't mind. My ensign is the sun and my brother the Sun of the Dust. The Dust Sun (Son) is shining through this darkness full of exhaust gas.

And what are you doing in this dozy day?

And by the way: thanks for changing my address. You have written "Askrikegarten" which more or less means a garden of ashes or an ash garden. But actually my address is Askrikegatan 13, which means e.g. the street of the ash kingdom, number 13.

Well, I don't mind. Now I can see a solar island at the horizon. And I can feel a dance time coming closer. I can see a dance in the sun...

PS. Some of my ribs still hurt. I was coughing too much in India.

Earth, 7 September

Is anybody living under your sway? Is somebody disturbing or obsessing you while you sleep?

Three days ago I was watching people while I was sitting at a café in Stockholm (King's Street). I celebrated Antonin Artaud's birthday ("We are not yet born, we are not yet of this world") and I listened to women (young women) who really had the gift of the gab. They talked about men, the new style (black coat and black trousers), bootlegs, the in-places, rendezvous (dates)... A clear transparent sunny afternoon and not too much traffic...

No road hogs or space men... But...

it happens that I feel shackled, imprisoned, unable to speak. I can also realize that the old world where the economy is the ruler (dictator) is on the brink of

115

bankruptcy... Russia, USA, Japan, China... Middle East... Well, you know: Who will take the blame? Fragmentation bombs, atomic bombs, poison bombs... and the oil business, Coca-Cola, hot dogs, and so forth...

"Mules!"

"What do you mean?"

"Do something for God's sake!"

"I can't..."

What kind of imagination is hiding behind all this emaciation, this lack of spirit?

In a dream the other night I saw three streams, three cataracts... Which one should I choose? which one was the safest? I was in a rowing-boat (a rowboat) and asked a man on a bank expecting some good advice. He didn't know, so I thought: the middle stream might be the best choice. Or maybe I ought to move upstream?

Back to reality. – Do you feel like a townie or like a country wench – or like a queen waiting for a coronation ceremony?

Cock-a-doodle-doo!

"But the still sama sitta", as James Joyce writes. Yes, not moving at all, but now and then: the way people move and celebrate... People here are soon going to vote, and I'm not a bad egg, I am not going to vote Conservative. I prefer the Green Party but should – as a matter of fact – like to start a Hildegard of Bingen party, a *viriditas*-party that celebrates and honours life instead of destroying it.

What a delirious world! Just look at the news or read Jack Kerouac's *Satori in Paris*. – Could you write *Satori in Stockholm*?

Continency, continents, contradictions... The other day a bus almost killed me on a zebra crossing. No, I didn't get knocked down, but it was a narrow escape. I had probably become too intoxicated with light that day.

Ups-a-daisy!

Some people talk about the return of the goddess, they are on a quest for the best, drink Green Phyto-Power and listen to the overtones in our space... In a dream somebody (maybe the philosopher Giordano Bruno) said: "In the eternal mind the world has never been created, but it is a creation. It will not end, nor start. But it is going on."

Now I am waiting for the wild song from the steppe.

21 September

In a letter I wrote at the beginning of September I told you about a dream where I asked somebody's advice. Could you advise me? Are you a good adviser? Is it advisable to live in the house of the rising sun, to fly the Atlantic, to forget about all the dreary days, to listen to the sea and a surge of choirs, to join the choir-singing, to talk (as perhaps Jack Kerouac did) to the Guardian of Purgatory, to pray to God for help, to avoid the bawdy blasphemers and the ridiculous news about Bill Clinton (the US President) and his harmless escapades, etcetera?

Once upon a time there was a little boy and a little girl... No, I am not going to tell a fairy tale and not a tale about hoodlums and nothing about the election that is going on... Peddlers, pederasts, pedestrians, a church exhibition, a fire performance in a church building, films: *Deep Impact, Armageddon...*

Yes, what can you expect in this time when the power of imagination is looking for a true source... And who can now trust all these cause-and-effect analyses when everybody (more or less) is feeling the presence of our human purgatory? Can the Goddess save us? Yes, the return of the Goddess has recently been manifested and celebrated in the archipelago outside Stockholm.

Do you sing and pray in the sun? do you dance and laugh together with your fellow countrymen? have you noted down your visions? Have you listened to Hildegard

117

of Bingen – her music and her songs? – "O Trinity, you are music, you are life."

Yes, sometimes I can hear a song that fills all the space. But I can't say who is singing and I don't know the creator of the song.

4 October (after having soaked in the bath)

It is possible I've occasionally been like a careless boy who dosen't bother to seek advice from wise people. Never mind... I will now try to do my best when there is a nip in the air... And if I had my way I should like to go back to the Middle Ages and speak Middle English and avoid cursing man's time on Earth.

Can you imagine that a great artist like Botticelli died in loneliness and oblivion!? Yes, even Mozart (the celestial, the heaven-stormer...) died almost in oblivion.

I'm not an erudite but I can remember Hamlet's words: "The time is out of joint: – O cursed spite, / That ever I was born to set it right."

I wonder: Is it still out of joint? And even more so than during Shakespeare's time?

Are you acquainted with Nikolai Berdyaev – a really remarkable freethinker. He talks about man's creative mission in a world where God's absence has been a riddle for a couple of centuries.

I've recently read his autobiography and admire his spiritual courage.

Autumn is here, the yellow leaves are falling and I shall soon give a discourse on Federico García Lorca and his poetry. – Yes, he was – as you know – an incredibly gifted poet, killed in 1936 by men obeying a blind power.

Yes, I got your card: "La Dame à la licorne: le goût, détail." You stayed a week in Paris and you paid a visit to the Cluny Museum. As a matter of fact this museum plays an important part at the end of my novel *The Red Knight and His Dreamed Worlds*. You can say it is a kind of initiation place in that book – that is a multidimensional story about pilgrims and penitents looking for their true missions on earth.

The snow has come, a winter world with snowdrifts and cold weather. I haven't seen the sun for weeks... "It's been a hard day's night..."

At the end of November I saw fire sculptures in a field not far from the house where I live. Yes, I could see how a sculpture called "the Sun Wheel" set fire to another sculpture called "The Mental Ice Age". I was witnessing how "the sun swallowed the winter wolves" and how "a new-born child's first breath" was manifested.

Finally "a new Phoenix" rose from the ashes and my Ash Kingdom became a more likable place to live in than it had been until then.

But I don't know... The energy we send out is coming back – isn't it? Our present society is full of mediums and wizards. But where is the truth, the faith, a firm decision, a piety that comes from our innermost being, our innermost heart?

Can we believe in a future where an enlightened humanity governs the world? I've just listened to a Tibetan monk (Palden Gyatso) telling about his thirty-three years long experience in Chinese prisons in Tibet. Medieval prison torture couldn't have been worse. His heartfelt meditation helped him to live through this atrocious suffering.

I will soon go to Lanzarote and stay there a couple of weeks. I need some new inspiration.

Let the healing energy descend. Be here. Drink volcano wine, be true to your mind, live in the sun, have some fun, absorb *prana* (energy) from a healing atmosphere... and let all light moments inspire you.

Yes. – I'm dancing on an island full of volcanoes. I'm on my path – *the Lion Path.*

And where are you?

What do you say about the seven rays?

1999: The Year of Destiny

Beyond the utmost borders, beyond all human history
and all the rest of the disasters of humankind, our life is
about to start.

Dear Shanti

A rainy day in January 1999

I am over the moon and I'm not losing heart although it's dark and I miss the sun, and sometimes I lose track of time when I feel I'm back on the Island of the Sun... Yes, I remember my recent stay on Lanzarote and my dance on the surface of volcanoes... No eruptions now. The last one took place in 1824...

I can remember my sun-greeting from a windmill on a black hill. I saw the sun set behind a mountain named Montaña de Saga while History kept its breath in a landscape that could be on the moon... I also remember the sound of my flute in a church dedicated to the Virgin of the Volcanoes – especially those called the Fire Mountains. Imagine all the volcanic cones and the black lava. – "Starting 16 million years ago, several eruptive phases of various degrees of intensity and duration have followed one another". – Yes, the earth is a living being, and ashes have been turned into life. A part of Lanzarote is now a farming area.

This island that I've visited before has inspired me to write a couple of chapters at the end of my novel *The History of the New Man. The Sign of Lazarus* (1995).

If you go there, don't forget to visit the Cactus Garden. Look at all the strange and absurd cacti, the porous volcanic grains, the colours, burnt sienna, black lava, tall black stones like statues... Yes, it's another world and still this world.

You also ought to visit the César Manrique Foundation at Taro de Tahiche (Lanzarote). This house is built over a lava river from an eruption (1730-36) and is a famous example of architecture that has been integrated with the environment. César Manrique, painter and landscape architect, was unfortunately killed in a car accident some years ago.

This year – 1999 – is a Wake-up-Year, I hope. And we need more abundance, more generosity... in Stockholm and elsewhere...

Thanks for your words about Paul Bowles and the drawing made by a child you probably know. Paul Bowles is not totally foreign to me. I've seen a film based on one of his novels. Not too bad... And I should like to read his novel *Up Above the World* (published 1966). He was married to the writer Jane Bowles – a remarkable woman, no doubt, strange and remarkable. You asked if he believed in love. I have to read him to find out. The film (based on one of his novels) I saw was a disillusioned story as far as I can remember. He lived and still lives, I think, in Morocco. But did he ever really understand the people of the desert?

City life can also be a kind of desert life. And on certain occasions I almost go up in the air when I see all these statues that once had a life. We need more nature, more moving quality, more space, more dance, more consideration... But how can you avoid all these rhinos? Sooner or later you run into a bull rhino in the underground, and I would say that it is a more unpleasant experience than to get a shove in the side by a wheel-barrow in a street jam at Har(i)dwar where you at least can meet and talk to holy people who believe in an omnipresent universal spirit.

Some days are sunny, some days you walk on air, you dance on air and feel as free as air... Today I've eaten at a restaurant called "Meaning Green". Good vegetarian food, tasteful setting, light, plenty of space...

Yes, I'm alive and kicking, but still in Sweden. Not much colour here, not much *duende* (guts)... A sleepy

atmosphere makes you sleepy... "Home is in Your Head."
... Engineering, mixing, synthesizers... rock, funk... or
Tibetan Buddhism or *A Month in the Brazilian
Rainforest*. Yes, that's real soul music: the rainforest.

I am dreaming and hoping and wandering and dancing
and listening... No, I will not go beserk. It is a marvellous
time. Now. This year: 1999.

PS. 1 March, after having seen *Othello* – a Shakespeare-
film by Orson Welles. – Othello says at the end of the
play: "Killing myself, to die upon a kiss." – Can such
things happen nowadays? What is love in this world
where villains and demi-devils rule? Is love a human goal
or even something beyond the fate of human beings?
Othello loved "not too wisely, but too well". – And what
about the love "that makes a man a fool" and drives him
mad?

I could say, *Speak of me as I am: a spokesman for the
Spring of Day.* – But it is not yet time for me to go. And I
don't want to be – as Othello says – "washed in steep-
down gulfs of liquid fire".

No singing birds can be heard at this very moment. The
snow is melting, the sun is shining, the air is rather
warm... Spring and the songbirds are approaching... The
sun of suns can be seen. Many people have open hearts
and can understand a new world that is knocking at the
door...

Do you remember James Joyce's words in his
Finnegans Wake: "Till daybowbreak and showshadows
flee. Thus be hek. Verily! Verily! Time, place!"?

In my not yet published book *Time Plays* and in all my
theatre work there are people coming from the future
meeting this time's consciousness. Especially when the
masters of this future society meet our time, there is a
clash. But the "showshadows" will flee...

Do you remember what happened to planet Earth 8000 years ago? I don't. Or do I? Did I live in a country called Sweden? I am not sure. And what did I do? Perhaps I tried to communicate... but did I succeed? Did I find the unshakeable race, the open-hearted people, the peace-minded souls? Who was I talking to? The angels? – Maybe. – Words used and misused... And sometimes: Silence.

Wars, warmongers, warplanes... They even killed small children in the year 1999... Why did they have to kill innocent life? Who was their god? Did they have any faith, any belief?

Many women tried to save their children and some were slain... How could soldiers behave in such a way? What was in the minds of the officers? I wish I knew.

Winters passed. Springs... Blackbirds were singing, crocuses bloomed... I talked now and then. I had some friends, I suppose. I wanted to save the jungles of the earth, the lakes, the rivers, the fir forests, the true poetry, the light in the darkest corners, the compassionate people, the bridge leading to the unshakeable race...

Had I chosen the right planet and the right time? Did I use the right tools, the right words?

I can hear a song that comes from nowhere and seems to know what I don't know, a song without words, a song on the steppe... I've heard it before, and I shall never forget it. It is coming closer... Maybe the time is near, maybe there is a message? something I have forgotten in the past? – But who is singing?

PS. in January 10 002... or April 1999 or... The dust of ages all around me. I'm trying to breathe in. Misery is prevailing and the Spirit probably hidden in the song of the blackbird. Who will raise the sleeper? Wounded and

126

still living. The tomb is empty and a distant cry can be heard. I believe I have to drink some living water in order to survive. I can feel the suffering everywhere and the sleeper must awaken.

A change of residence, emigration...?... No, at least not now. How small it's all, and still: Great.

"Breathe, breathe the exile air and feel the luminous water giving you a new strength. You are sitting on a lush hill in a rainforest listening to the crickets and the frogs. Refugees, blood, killing, prisons, tears... belong to the past. The voices of the rainforest are now your best friends, and you can feel their healing power.

"Balance and harmony. Inspiration.

"Living Water."

Yes, that's what the voice tells me. Whose voice?

Before the year of 2000

No, I never went to Smara, a desolate town in a desert south of Morocco, I never saw the walls and the black stones, but I have felt the desert wind on my way to the town of Ouarzazate, on the threshold to Sahara South. I remember the wind and the stillness, the absolute silence in a desert of almost red cliffs... I could hear my heart beating while I was meditating in a small valley under a bright blue sky. The only sound was my heartbeats and my breath – in a universe full of riddles. No camels round about, no herdsmen... Here time ends. Life's drab faces and poor mishaps belong to a forgotten past. I might have been living on a planet called Earth a million years or more. I don't care. I don't exist in time any more. Time is a delusion. Who cares about ages after the final step? Tongues are undoubtedly still talking about Timbuktu's burning sands, about war and peace and suffering and bomb sites... Yes, they were slow in learning. They kept on repeating the same mistakes – from morning until night.

Now and then I used to drum, and I played the flute together with snake charmers. Vastness, *médinas*, blue-painted doors, tea beside a shed in a warm summer wind not far from the sea...

Bitter time, bitter fruits, bitter herbs... a slackness in the spirit or no spirit at all... Clouds, cloudy and sleeping minds, drifting on the ocean of sleep... But now I can hear: the music, an open-air concert at a desert theatre, a quite well-preserved ruin in a desert world. Flutes and drums and singing voices. I lie down and listen. Perhaps I can find somebody whom I can speak to before it is too late. It is afternoon. The sun is shining and the music is there: not far away.

PS. I often dream of desert landscapes, the Atlas foothills, crenellated red walls, dignity and indignity... Man against Destiny in a desert full of silence... Who is talking in the universe, who, and why? writing and talking and walking and killing?... Who? And why?

Choirs, solos, winds, storms... And suddenly a whisper you can hardly hear, telling about some mysterious feeling, a perfume, a fragrance you cannot catch.

This day is called *imix* in Mayan. *Ximi, imix, ixim...*

It is a May day. The other day I told a publisher: "I am not a god on earth, but I might be able to work miracles if I have to in order to survive." – A green day. Sun. Cherry blossoms. I have to do the cooking. – "We have the useful arts and we have the liberal arts." – I'm reading *Stephen Hero* by James Joyce, who published "nothing but masterpieces" according to the *Times Literary Supplement*. I don't know if I agree. But at least *Finnegans Wake* is a masterpiece. And I have to add: an epiphany. – "Clogan slogan. Quake up, dim dusky, wook doom for husky!"

128

At the crossroads where the new heavens are meeting
I am sending you my solar greetings.

A week ago: arrival in Lima, Peru. I wrote: "Night, songs,
a strange city full of cars (the wrong ones). Having been
without sleep for almost 20 hours... Now reading Tagore:
'Oh human heart.' – Feeling my heartbeats and the petrol
stench in the rather chilly air. Music (catchy songs) all
around. – *The Kentucky Fried Chicken* – a café. What a
place for a vegetarian! The Hotel Eiffel, where I stay, is
close to the Club Waikiki.

"Sleep my baby: 207 days to the year 2000. Mankind
will supposedly go on sleeping or... will an awakening
take place this year?

"Every word is a world. Has anybody understood the
meaning of being here on Earth? – Year 2000; 20 000;
200 000...?... What kind of bodies do we have in the year
200 000? Bird bodies, perhaps?"

And now?

Well, that was a week ago. Now in the white and warm
sunshine in Cuzco I've witnessed the Corpus Christi
Festival – many saints, dragons, drums, dances,
trumpets... The Inti Raymi Festival will come off within a
fortnight. I suppose you have seen or read about the
Inca Winter Solstice Festival when the Inca (Inka) is
holding up a chalice towards the sun. *Inti* means sun in
Quechua (the Inca language).

3300 meters above sea level I can see the pure white
snow, the holy mountain, the "Star of Snows". Can you
imagine Indians carrying heavy ice-blocks 7-8 kilometres
from the holy mountain Ausangate all the way to Cuzco?

Today I've seen children dancing and the solar temple
Intihuasi (Coricancha). I stood behind the Navel of the

Earth greeting the sun together with an initiated Inca Indian.

The other day I told a taxi-driver that I was a poet. He knew more Quechua than Spanish. – "Please write me a poem," he said. I told him that I could not do it very well in Spanish. But after a while some words came to me:

La vida no es sueño.
La vida no es dinero.
La vida es sol.*

Not a very good poem, I imagine. But you can say it is an attempt to express myself in a tongue you know but I cannot say I master at all... I can get along, that's all...

Night again. Voices from the street. The world sleeps. The rainforest is not far away... The solar power time is coming closer...

Save the true poetry!

Save the air, the water, the forests...

Yes, people – at least some – are acting in an enlightened way...

All
Good
Inca
Solar
Wishes

PS. At the village Pisac's Sunday market a boy wanted to sell a painting to me. He said: *"Un buen precio."* – I said: *"No es posible comprar el sol."* – He answered: *"El Sol es mi Dios."* – But who is God in this time? – *Dinero* (money)? – Or the pure water of a virgin spring?

---

*Life is not a dream. / Life is not money. / Life is sun.

Machu Picchu, Peru.

Time may be a heap of dust, an incredible hunger, humiliations, suffering... But it goes on and on... Arrival, departure, fill in, fill up... Who are you? Nobody, no doubt – in the immense light whose origin nobody knows.

Some days ago I wrote: "Hot July night in Madrid. – I wonder: Who is sponsoring time? Who is time's ruler? Who is time's servant? I wish I could express the truth of the squeaking wheels, of the lost people, of the poor... of the rich... *'Siempre Domingo'*... *'El juego de las lunas'*... The black bulls, the matadors *en sombra y sol.*"

A couple of weeks ago I wrote: "I don't scurry. I am at Ollantaytambo, Peru. Ollantay is a name of an Inca warrior. Tambo means 'lodge for resting'.

"I am not staying at a lodge; no, I am staying at an inn called Las Orquídeas. Have I been in a rut? I've talked to walls and statues. (Do you recall my play – *The Night of the Statues*?) And I have certainly been pounding the pavements of the world... What is now springing to my mind? – On 19 June I wrote: 'I am sitting at the foot of Machu Picchu, in a village called Aguas Calientes. I enjoy the warm noon sun two days before the Winter Solstice.'"

Time may be a hard labour, a cry for survival, a degrading suffering... But it goes on and on... Pain can be turned into joy. Although you often meet people who are not your type. I cannot stand sergeant-like security controllers – e.g. at Arlanda airport. Sensitiveness and subtleness are rare qualities. What can we expect of the future?

Transgressions and offences are commonplaces... But what do you say about Indians carrying heavy ice-blocks from a holy place in the Andes? They are devoted pilgrims who believe in the power of a holy rock and the power of the ice from a holy mountain.

The year 2000 is approaching and mankind can look back on thousands of years of maltreatment: body, mind, and soul. Life has not yet started. Man is not yet born. He is a shadow in the realm of shadows. The light of Poetry can sometimes penetrate into the Valley of Darkness. But on the whole...?...

The sunrise experience together with Indian shamans beside a fertility altar on the top of Machu Picchu is an event I will never forget.

You have certainly seen pictures of the majestic and awe-inspiring mountains round the cosmic site called Machu Picchu. The greeting of the sun at sunrise 21 June (winter solstice) the year 1999 at this cosmic place in the Andes was of a very special value. You could call it a harmonic convergence. An Egyptian and European solar tradition met an Indian solar initiation. An Indian shaman performed a purifying rite and I played the flute. He told me about his art of becoming weightless and mentioned the signs of a couple of condors... You can be initiated through water, through earth, through fire... You need holy temples, holy mountains... But do you need polluted cities?

The old polluting technology will soon be gone, I hope. The new fuels are water, air, solar power... You know about the solar cells. Now the French engineer Guy Nègre has developed "a concept of a totally non-polluting engine for urban areas. This invention uses high pressure compressed air..."

I didn't ask the Andean water oracle why I am here on this earth in this universe. Never mind. It must go on. I have to go on existing and creating and breathing and dancing... To breathe is an important part of our creation. – To breathe and move in freedom – is that the normal state of being in the future?

Stockholm's summer heat is filling my studio. The balcony door is open. The sky is clear. The sun: brilliant.

Now I remember a beggar boy whom I met in Cuzco, Peru, during the celebration of Corpus Christi. He came up to me where I was standing beside a cathedral's main entrance. He wanted a gift, a coin, and noticed a badge a badge-seller had sold to me (or almost forced me to buy). On the badge you could see Christ carrying the cross on his Via Crucis. The beggar boy wanted the badge and got it. I remember the words: *Via crucis via lucis.* Anyhow the boy didn't mind the burden. And perhaps it was light for him... I have got enough of burdens and want to be as light as a condor soaring in the sky above Machu Picchu.

PS. 12 July. Thanks for your Monument Valley card! You asked if I've published a new book. – Yes, *Time Plays*: 52 numbered copies.

Shall I send you a copy? Are you in Toronto in July and August?

17 July the year?

Is this the year 3000 or the year 2012? Tell me, what did you do 1000 years ago? Burning your incense, laughing on the path to mastery, writing letters of love...?... And what did I do?

Did I have a fondness for dancing? *Yes.*

I wonder: Did Akhenaton (Akhenaten, Echnaton...) dance?

Some scholars or researchers (e.g. Ahmed Osman) even believe that Akhenaton *is* Moses.

But who cares? Who are you in this inhibited Western culture? Or in the immense light whose origin nobody knows? I rather listen to the sound of the rain than to the words from the big guns. I prefer trees to money, and I know that money doesn't grow on trees, as they say. But a crown of a tree in a well-kept orchard is a living miracle – and what is money in the mind of a miser?

People work, they are sweating their guts out, and what do they earn? Who are the profiteers? Not the poets, anyhow. Will the spirit of the sun (of Aton) change everybody's mind one day? This year? Next year...?...

Amendments, improvements... The work must go on in this wilderness. Now I can remember a shaman who talked to me about condors soaring above Machu Picchu – heavenly birds whose message he could read, a message about weightlessness, and I said something about a solar truth penetrating all dark veils, about solar words never understood before on this planet... It is late, almost too late, and I am still a prisoner... But the heavens are changing and the earth will not allow the old lies to continue...

Stocks and stock-markets... No, that's not my world. A river, a wind, a primeval forest, a windmill, a real human meadow or garden has a greater value (or worth) according to my taste.

And if this is the year 2012 or 3000, I say, I must not forget all the living souls, the Work must go on, I'll go on.

13 August

In some churches (e.g. in Scotland) they say: "As it was in the beginning, is now, and ever shall be: world without end."

Some days ago I was in Edinburgh during a fringe theatre festival; I saw e.g. *Water Carriers* (a dance performance) and Sarah Finch as the woman in Samuel Beckett's play *Not I* (stage : Saint Mary's Cathedral).

Before seeing *Not I* (in an excellent interpretation) I had lunch at a café called Délifrance, where I read: "A small but potent coffee served black characterized by a flavour and an aroma so intense they bite."

On 11 August I saw the solar eclipse outside Rosslyn Chapel (near Edinburgh). The sky was clear and the eclipse was almost total.

135

I greeted the meeting of the sun and the moon.

The time of the fifth sun is now past history – according to the Aztecs. – In England they say that "the shrinking sun shone like silver".

The moon shadow went from the West to the East. The West shook the East awake.

Everything was very calm outside Rosslyn Chapel built more than five hundred years ago by Sir William Saint Clair (an ancestor).

Now it is 13 August, the Day of Destiny. The time of the Aztec Sun Stone Calendar ends today – some people say.

From now on I intend to steer my own life ship, my own destiny, my work in a sunlight that is free of charge. The falsity of the world's words and the world's works is not my business.

In the outer stream of our daily reality the true story of our life is more or less hidden. Who is not hiding the truth? Who can say: "My life has never started and it will never end."

This day, 13 August 1999, has been a sunny day in Paris, a peak season tourist city, full of wrong cars and high tourist prices.

Somebody staying at the bookshop Shakespeare and Company asked me, when he was informed about my book where Quetzalcoatl speaks: "Did you channel his words?" I answered: "No. I just wrote on different levels – sometimes noticing what happened around me, sometimes using a heightened awareness..."

The true reality is always multidimensional, but it is not always easy to listen to an inner voice while the civilization around you is roaring.

PS. I've written this letter at the restaurant Le Grenier de Notre-Dame, and now I'm going back to my studio at the Hôtel Chamonix.

A young man called Nathan asked me in a park not far from Notre-Dame in Paris if I wanted to have some horoscope guide lines (the Mexican way). – "No," I said, "I would only feel embarrassed. I prefer to follow my intuition, my inner voice."

He didn't get disappointed. He said he respected my opinion.

I talked to him about the freedom in Bram van Velde's paintings, paintings that could have been made by a child – or rather: an eternal and enlightened child.

"Tell me your date of birth," he said.

I answered:

"I have no birthday."

And it is true. All birthdays seem to have lost all meanings in my thinking. What is birth and what is death? – Borders, certainly; but nothing more.

Inside Notre-Dame I saw the stained-glass rose windows. What a creation! They reminded me of Buddhist mandalas. In the darkness of the cathedral I could meditate and see the inner light. And as you know: I detest the noisy and dangerous traffic and the petrol fume. I prefer air cars and hydrogen gas cars. If Paris were full of these cars it would be a paradise.

Bookstalls, doves, a long queue outside Notre-Dame, a beggar woman... *the day of the Second Coming.*

I stayed for a couple of days at the Hôtel Esmeralda, but not in "la chambre des rois". Have you read Victor Hugo's book on Esmeralda? I mean the book about the bell-ringer of Notre-Dame and the gypsy woman – Esmeralda. In fact: not a real gypsy. It is a romantic, realistic, and tragic novel.

I walked the streets – and mostly: the quiet ones, e.g. Rue Mouffetard and Rue Descartes. I sat down at La Chope (Place de la Contrescarpe) and watched the people. Lots of tourists everywhere: smoking, drinking, chatting, gossiping, photographing, observing, discussing, waiting for somebody...

I also waited.

When does this somebody come?

Who is she? Who is he?

Judith, Ivana, George, Luke... Who are they?

I asked: *Is my salvation approaching*? I looked at the doves in the trees, the poplars, the sky, the sun, the purple clouds... *the Second Coming*... The incarnated masters are finally helping you to the true wine, the true words.

I thought: This is France, Paris, a sunny and warm August week; this is the heart of Europe, this is the world: the bookshop Shakespeare and Company – George, Luke... the book people full of thoughts, languages, and dreams... and a tradition to maintain since the time of James Joyce's new wordings and "rejoycings".

I told a girl who had read Marguerite Duras and wept on almost every page about my reading at Shakespeare and Company. I read from *Time Plays* and at least Judith and Ivana understood and liked it. It was a beautiful evening, 19 August 1999.

All Creation was there. The purple clouds, the sunlight lighting up (illuminating) Notre-Dame, the silent wings in the air...

The Second Coming.

But where is Judith now? Where is Ivana?

I said to the girl who was selling her small paintings: "Sooner or later I shall float in the air and speak the tongue of the angels." – Yes, I can feel the presence of a time without money-people and bill-people. Pay and you are accepted. Don't pay and you are a criminal.

The old time has been loaded with conventions, weapons, stodginess, and hair-trigger alert. Fairly often: a damn stupid world ruled by idiots. It is almost impossible to be respected today if you are without money.

I remember the village Saint-Clair-sur-Epte, the holy well, the healing water, the saint – Saint-Clair – who was beheaded more than a thousand years ago... I can also remember the engrailed cross in the unfinished Rosslyn Chapel in Scotland, and I have read about Sir William St Clair, the builder of the chapel and a very learned man. But most of all I recall all the pictures of the black sun, the darkening sky in the middle of the day, the people watching the sky... *the Second Coming*... All over Europe: a silence, a darkness, a feeling of awe...

We are here in a Creation we can't catch. Soon the dumbness will end, soon the heavens will talk...

In the Bible you can read (Matthew 24:30): "And then shall appear the sign of the Son of man in heaven: and then shall all the tribes of the earth mourn, and they shall see the Son of man coming in the clouds of heaven with power and great glory." – In an English newspaper (12 August 1999) I read: "Through the portal to the heavens the crescent-shaped sliver of the shrinking sun shone like silver before it harrowed and was stuffed. Then the Moon's shadow raced in across the sea from the west, bringing down a curtain of darkness which drew cheers and gasps from the people."

What is happening in your life? Where have you been in July and August? I got a card from Monument Valley – but that was a couple of months ago. In a dream the other night I dreamt about a landscape that looked like Monument Valley. I saw red rocks, peaks, a valley... I held a big boulder in place on a mountain ridge. I heard somebody mentioning the name *Utah*. The boulder was almost coming loose and was a danger for people walking down below... Finally I got the help I needed: a woman climbed down to my place and she helped me to underprop the stone so it could stay where it was.

It was in the nick of time I got this help. Now there is a hope for the future...

PS. I've put aside a copy of *Time Plays*. Shall I send it to your Toronto address?

23 September

Somebody who saw my first exhibition (at an art gallery in Stockholm) wrote:

"Paintings, pain things... The experience was and is wonderful." That person also wrote (as a summing up): "The avian invasion from the ninth dimension explodes the birth of an eye in our soul."

Who has said:

"I am here to create the world. As far as I know the world has not yet been created. We have not yet known life. Life has not yet been discovered. We are still groundlings, afraid of the endless dimensions, the time-less and immense sky."

A voice in my dream? And maybe I've said something like that in some of my previous letters.

At times I listen to a distant call. – "Are you there? Do you hear me, do you understand...?..."

No answer.

She is still sleeping, and now I can remember the pain that pierced the very marrow of my bones...

A whole world pricked by a poisoned spindle and sent to sleep – is that a reality? In a dream I have asked:

"Can you hear me? I am here. What offer have you made? What do you give me?"

Who can like Job repent in dust and ashes?

Do you hear the earth? Do you hear the dream of Destiny? A predatory mankind exists. But is there a predestination, a Fate you cannot avoid? Maybe there has been. But will there be? – In the sun on the sky bridge I can see new worlds approaching: a dance time, a time when everybody is full of fun in the sun, or could be?

The autumn is here. The sky is cloudy today; it is raining and I am dreaming of a sunny fairyland. I need some money and a theatre where I can stage my plays. I hope to be able to go to Guatemala in November or December. What plans do you have?

29 October

Thanks
      for your
letter!
      Night just now.
      Work. Sleep. Dreams...
      Hope.

☆

Do you think I've finished my first Shanti book? Or should I add something in 2000? – Yes, I think I have to.

A whole era – 2000 years – in darkness – more or less.

And what will now happen?

I'll send you *Time Plays* under separate cover.

A new edition (slightly revised and better published) will be printed next year.

It's a new way of publishing... Yes, I know. But it is a must. We have to breathe new life into the new millennium. I am not losing heart.

What about your work? And how do you feel in your new home?

In this Year of Destiny I've asked: "Why has man in this life a fate? What rules?"

2000: The Year of Mary Magdalene

We are passing the border of time at this very moment. The wall of time is not our prison any more. We belong to a time that plays. The universe is our playground.

(13 October 2000)

Dear Shanti

Flores, Guatemala, 31 Dec. 1999 – 2 Jan. 2000

Soon it's all over... The old, dark, inhuman, cruel, and inglorious millennium.

And as you know: I don't long for the darkness and the wintry cold in Stockholm and Europe.

"From where are you?" people ask.

"From the universe, the inverse, the multiverse..."

"You must be known in your own home country."

"No. I'm not known – or well-known – in any country."

"But you've written and published books?"

"Well, I have. More than 20 – as a matter of fact."

"You have readers. Many?"

"I don't know. Never seen any or met any... Or to be honest: one or two... but not many... so far..."

"And now, tell me: What are your plans? What are you up to?"

"No idea. I'm listening to a voice I've lost, a jungle voice, the wilderness voice, a holy voice, holy drums, flutes, and a wild singing – almost from another dimension."

☆

The Caribbean sea is waiting – the islands where you don't have to inhale the noxious fumes from cars and buses made by a lunatic uncivilized spirit that soon will pass away, I hope.

We already have hydrogen cars, air cars, electric cars... and maybe one day: magnetic cars.

What in creation would you say about our war history full of creative human ability?

Tomorrow I'll be in the Tikal jungle where you e.g. can see the Giant Jaguar Pyramid. On the plaza between two

145

Maya Tikal pyramids I should like to stage my play *The Last Night of the Body* (not yet translated into English)... The drums, the dance, colourful living souls and black ghosts... Finally – after the end of the funeral – a new sunrise hidden in the almost forgotten dreams of a lost world that has lost its true voice...

I can now hear new voices singing a song that opens a consciousness behind consciousness... behind... and giving birth to a tongue that is as fresh as crystal-clear mountain spring water...

You are maybe in a spruce forest. I am in a jungle... or I shall be... and then the Caribbean sea... the island of Caye Caulker, the barrier reef... the eternal revolution, the creative spirit without end and beginning...

I listen to a small waterfall and can see the sun shining on Lake Petén Itzá.

Soon the Sun will set.

A millennium is gone.

> *Solar*
> *millennium*
> *greetings*

PS. 2 January 2000 in the tropical heat. What do you say today about mankind's politics, economy, well-doing...?... Are people healing our Mother Nature, are they putting an end to wars between nations, etcetera, creating a real global green peace?

I said something like that to a blond girl (a backpacker) from a nation in the Near East. I met her a couple of hours ago outside a bank in the little town of Santa Elena.

"Greenpeace...?... No," she answered. "We must have real peace in the Near East. I should like to go into politics in order to be able to create this kind of peace."

"What do you mean? – Green?"

"No. Real."

"But green is real. Nature is real. Air, earth, water... are real... Human weapons are unreal, at least they are not organic green..."

But to her the world was red, black, white... and not green...

In the tropical restaurant garden with *hamacas* – where these words are written – a parrot is talking. His name is Serafino, and he is green. He likes a peaceful green Maya-world and Green Peace. He wants to "reform industrialism and secure peace".

Maya gold
wishes

3 February

Can I really exist in a city world where the soul is a prisoner in a dark dungeon, where life is a forgotten tale that nobody reads or hears about? Can I breathe in this prison where imagination has lost its wings and the fear of a free spirit is a warder I can't talk to...?...

No, I can't...

So what am I doing here? Have I landed on the wrong planet? a petrol stinking planet, a nuclear mad planet?

Well, I don't know. But I know you rarely find a true knowledge of real theatre, of true catharsis and true rhythm. I now recall a real traditional Maya-mask-dance-theatre I've seen in the evergreen rainforest of Guatemala. There they still preserve some knowledge of the importance of a true footstep, of ground steps beating the drum, Mother Earth.

But here death is prevailing...

Or am I wrong?

Before I left Cancún I happened to meet a young man who took care of several lions. He knew what a living energy is; he knew that all crucified souls must resurrect one day; yes, he even probably knows that Creation is an everlasting miracle and that the traitors, the death mongers, in Europe and elsewhere, will not be able to go on with their business forever...

The Funeral has had its time.

I can also recollect a meeting with Tarzan's (Johnny Weissmuller's) daughter, Lisa. We talked about the Egyptian sign of life (*ankh*) – a sign I am wearing on a silver chain round my neck. If you know how to breathe, you know how to live. The tragic situation of man is that he has lost most of the original art of breathing. But it can be remedied, don't you think? We know pretty well the rottenness and the corruption and the ditchwater manners that are now acclaimed in some places... But everything has an end – even the worst hell (Sweden or SW of Eden, and so forth). The Dawn will come and the Sun will break through...

Spring Equinox in Europe

Dear
    solar
        sister

A voice – that I've heard in my dreams – brings peace to my heart and that voice is what the world needs. – Is it your voice?

Now and then I have asked myself: "Have I taken my hogs to the wrong market?"

My time is an enigma, my life, my work... our work...?...

Once I said to you: "Our time together is world history." – But at present I am at a loss.

I should like to know more about your dreams and be able to read your creative writing.

Can I read you as though I read a book? Can I see your fear, your need of space... and the power directing our whole play? – I do wish I could.

Do you know me? Have you seen my history, my non-history, my time beyond all times, my age beyond all ages?

Where were you when I stayed in the desert trying to find traces or vestiges of your existence on earth, when I heard a whisper that could have been your voice, when I felt your breath without hearing it in a universe that is created by the song you always sing in your deepest mind and in the songs you have already composed and in the new songs we are creating together?

Everybody is perhaps – in a way – alone in the universe without end. And yet...?... You have the new Maya vision – *maya* means illusion; but the Maya land is a reality, and there (and anywhere) the sun and the moon can meet...

PS.

The heart of the matter is
The heart that matters
And all my fetters are gone in
This letter to your heart's
Innermost soul...

Do you hear a call? Somebody calling
You from afar, as if you had listened
To a star or something behind all walls...

Calls, distant calls, telling you what I am.
Who am I? And you? Not just circulations or
Imagination or bodies and souls in a world
Rising in rebellion, roaring like a wild sea...
You and me here for the first time on a stage

That needs our presence, our essence, our spirit,
Our voices, bodies, light and healing...

And now I wonder: How are you feeling?

Sweden in April

Use your noddle! Pass the hat round! – Yes, you know: all
this muck, television hostesses, suppression, small-
mindedness, and so on*... Really humiliating. But what
can we do? A lot of money here and there, but a spiritual
bottom layer. The end-and-rebeginning is at hand, but
first: "onegugulp down of the nauseous forere
brarkfarsts" (Joyce in *Finnegans Wake*). – The world is
in the mire; we know that. And some hearts are on fire.
When will Ascension Day be a reality for everybody?
When will my miracle plays (initiation plays) be
televised? An immense scream without end is in my view
a justifiable answer to all stupidity and insensitiveness.
   I suppose you remember the secret mission we've
been talking about. It is a story beyond time and
includes the first beings and humankind's cultures and
civilizations on earth. A moment before passing through
the time space sluice I said to you:
   "We shall see our true being beyond the time space veil
when life has passed through the door of death creating
an everlasting gospel of playful waves."
   I can also remember a twinge of pain and then a
blackout. What had happened? what happened? I saw
the earth and the flight line, the Mission Control Centre,
and I believe we touched down... Anyhow we didn't
splash down... And here we are again trying to express
in human tongues some fragments of a reality we have
almost forgotten.

*Alluding to a TV-appointment.

150

I ought to bring in an indictment against a so-called civilized world that has lost its uplifting sense of humour and decorum. Man has turned into a mad monkey devouring himself. Or am I wrong? Is an ascension movement giving birth to an entirely new society? No gurus anywhere but a world where inspired poetry is revered as in olden times.

Jungle sounds are now all around me. I feel at home. I can breathe, and I listen to the cries of the howlers. Outside my windows: a bleak and cold spring. But I don't mind; times are a-changing and I can feel your presence in your absence...

Holy Week 2000

Believe me or not: I am still here on this planet, in this universe, in this multiverse... Sometimes I wake up in the middle of the night when I hear your singing voice. I hear it within myself and you are somewhere else.

Last night I came in a dream to a seashore, saw the beaches, talked to some people and went up on a small mountain. From there a narrow path took me down to a rocky and many-coloured valley where I heard polyrhythmic sounds, voices, songs – a strange and yet very familiar kind of music. But I didn't find any beach any more and wanted to return to the top of the mountain. I saw steps leading up to the top and saw people coming down. I asked two women and a man the way to the steps and climbed a big boulder to find out... Then – when I stood on the boulder – I saw the crucified body of Christ like a shadow in front of me. I turned in another direction. But the shadow that reminded me of a drawing by Saint John of the Cross was still there. *In front of me.* But not only one shadow. My own shadow was almost overlapping the shadow of the Master. And where was the body in reality? What did this all mean? Which power was behind this shadow play? I could only guess and felt I had to move on. I slided down from the top of the big boulder, saw a crashed glider but no pilot. In the distance I could see people coming down the steps. I looked at the almost rust-red ground and tried to forget the shadow of the crucified body still haunting in my mind. Somehow I knew that I had to get to the top of the mountain and perhaps meet somebody I could talk to. The waste and – to some extent – magic land round me was not my real home. But I liked the songs I had heard, and maybe they where coming from another world.

My cacti are blooming. The sky is grey. It is almost silent. No singing of birds. Motor traffic at some distance off. What are people doing? Watching TV?

Is this moment an everlasting gospel of a never-ending beginning? The cactus flowers speak to me. They seem to be happy.

PS. Wednesday in Holy Week. It's Easter – or almost Easter. Are you celebrating the Passover and also eating the Passover? God, they say, once spared the Israelites in Egypt. And what happened to Benjamin – the sun (son) of the right hand?

Do you know that the Gothic cathedrals in Europe are supposed to have been formed in honour of Mary Magdalene and the *hieros gamos*? The time is coming closer, the *hieros gamos*-time when the male and the female will meet again and form a wholeness, when people don't need to eat sacred mushrooms in order to see the sacred earth and their mission on this earth. Sun and moon will meet like in your song and this will heal the wound of Time.

I can see you and yet I cannot see you, but I hear your voice over the mountains, across the steppe, above the sea... And this voice is guiding me. Sooner or later I shall find my home and a reunion will take place on an awakening earth...

Do you know our fate? Do you know the truth?

PPS. Good Friday. No. The crucifixion will not continue to be the true symbol of man's history. I believe we can create something else. Don't you? We start now. Time will tell... And I am now listening to bells from the deep... and to a tone of a voice that is as natural as Mother Nature herself. You are singing... and the birds and the flowers... Yes, the whole spring is waking up after a long and cold and degrading night.

29 April at night

Is your work your dream or your dream your work? Are you still working together with the aborigines?

Perhaps our civilization as a whole is going to the dogs and becoming a scrap heap. What is your opinion?

I know that this is an everlasting moment in a non-ending time. But who is directing? Who is shaping this life? Who is behind it all? Is there anything behind? I mean: Who is the ruler?

I must say I often disagree with the ruler. But in exceptional cases I give my consent.

A couple of weeks ago I was out in the wilds and caught a cold. I feel out of sorts, but never mind... I don't care. The solar storms have been very intense this year and people in Stockholm have seen red northern lights at night. The grand alignment of planets in our solar system is coming closer. Everywhere they talk about 5 May – the alignment day.

Spring is here. Blackbirds are singing. Bills must be paid, the food, the rent... And I don't want to live in a tent... dreaming of abundance, heaven on earth, the kingdom of heaven.

Where are all my playmates gone?... They are rare of course: the children of the sun. I met some in Peru. And now I am waiting for the Virgin: She who descends from the region of light and makes me feel at home on this earth.

May the May spring be with you and all the planets guide you through the morning star portal.

Whitsun 2000

Somewhere in the Bible you can read that your body is the temple of the Holy Ghost. But what is the Holy Spirit? Does any human being know? Can anybody tell? People sing: "Go, tell it on the mountain!" – And now in Stockholm a gospel choir from Atlanta, Georgia, USA, sings: "Holy Ghost, Holy Ghost, Holy Ghost..." And people in the King's Garden dance and sing and pay homage to God by their dance and their singing... Even I did dance and I am – as you know – a dancer since time immemorial.

But who am I? Who are you? Who are we?

I listen and I hear:

"I am nobody in a body not yet revealed. For that reason I can be everywhere without being anywhere. My time is a miracle beyond all historical ages... Seen and still not seen... An old oak tree in Galilee might know. But who could tell in the midst of hell. And yet, aren't we all creators belonging to a never-ending creation? – The clouds have been dark, but now they are gone. The sun is strong, and people walk and talk about the crucifixion era, an era that has ended – at least in some individuals' minds, thoughts, and actions."

You hear, you listen, you say:

"You squelch in the mud and don't see that a new heaven (haven) is descending to those who have passed the borderline and old blind dogmas and creeds and now can rejoice with Joyce and all other true writers and poets – a rejoicing in an air without pollution."

154

Pollution or not... Anybody knows that false bodies and a false spirit have ruled too long. And when somebody asks me in a green garden: "How old are you?" – I answer: "I am getting younger." – "But tell me now: How old?" – "An eternity. At least." – And so forth... until all men realize that they have been serving as slaves, working in the mire of a slave time. But what will happen when the Spirit starts to talk and dance in Everybody?

Midsummer 2000

Where did I meet you? Did I meet you? Have we ever met? Shall we meet – in the year 2000, in the year ZERO, in the year...?...

"I request the pleasure of the company of...?..."

I am sorry, I've lost the track, I've lost all tracks... I don't know where I live, where I am, who I am... I don't mind. Even the battlefields belong to a memory I don't care about.

Joyce writes: "A virgin, the one, shall mourn thee." Where is she? In which distant past did I feel her presence? Did she... finally appear after the old era had breathed its last? *Yes.* No reason to be in mourning now... And then the dance in the open air – the great Opening in the Opening?

Yes.

At the end of my composition *Civilization – a Purgatory* the following words (here translated into English) are uttered by a whispering voice: "And the townsfolk down below were surprised by the scream, the piercing scream of the god." – A sentence taken from the long epic prose poem *Vents* (Winds) by Saint-John Perse.

Now I listen to my inner voice and can hear: "The virgin, the one, shall be what you are. She is already here waiting for the opening of a new era's day." – But can I see her? Have I already met her? Did she – as I did –

listen to the demanding and uplifting music by Karlheinz Stockhausen at Skinnskatteberg, a village in a province not far from Stockholm? Yes, I really liked *Kathinka's Chant* and *Oktophonie*. The critic of one of the biggest newspapers in Sweden didn't like it at all. But who is this critic? How does he listen? What is hiding in the deepest recesses of his innermost mind?

World music or not world music? That is not the question. The bodies of men are tones or notes in a space-time we have not yet understood. Man's tone language is changing. When he truly knows his senses and can read space as a simple book he will also be able to master a tone language that is healing. Time and space will meet and a new man will be created.

"Blather," says the expert, the critic. "Mushe, mushe of a mixness," says Joyce and laughs. Who can say: "Forgive them all their faults."?

I can see a humorous twinkle in the eyes of a wise man looking at the world's struggle to understand itself and the art that is taking its first steps in an immense space.

But you are here, aren't you? In a light-coloured dress. Yes, Ana, Amazia, Plurabelle, Natasha... I shall soon know your true name and your gait, your voice and your silence... It is midsummer. Cloudy sky. It is not raining. It will rain...

It is the year 2000, and man is fast asleep until the time of resurrection gives him a light that lifts him up to his true destination and brings about his rightful feeling of presence in a universal creation process.

In the year ZERO

No, I cannot say I am in the city, the bodies there are too heavy, too lost... They are knocking into people and joining the night play that soon will end... I am now flashing a signal to you. Can you feel it? Out here on the moor I cannot see if you are flashing back. I may have lived in this isolation during centuries. I have no notion of what time it is. Everything in the garden is lovely... No, not always, but sometimes. Fruits and vegetables and spring water... I don't need much. I talk to a few birds, a fox, a rabbit... They are human enough. I still remember the battlefields and people's tongues. But are they real? I mean: people and their tongues. I must admit they were inventing and creating all the time. Mostly rubbish, I should say. And most of them seemed to be afraid of something. Of themselves, probably. And of love, of light, of life... Strange creatures, aren't they?

Tell me, how do you spend your days? What is in your mind, in your dreams? Have you got into a habit of being a stranger among other strangers?

The whole fabric of society must be reshaped. Yes, we know that. Once you said: "Love is the force that keeps the Universe going." Do you feel the same thing right now? And what kind of love do you mean? Flash me a signal if you have time! Let me know what people are doing. Are they really happy? Do they love themselves and the earth?

I do miss you. But I know that you are on the way... and I hope to meet you in the garden again. Then a new solar play can start. My birds are telling me that.

PS. I must say I like to feel and listen to your breathing. It's telling me a lot about your soul's history. Perhaps your soul is my true home?

PPS. You know you are the still moment living in an eternal life where history has ended.

Here is a secret message to you:

The lion heart will dance
once you penetrate the veils of time
and behold the right face and body
of eternal creation...

Now time has come for the Virgin Bride
to descend
so a meeting can take place
and a wholeness be created.
The *hieros gamos* rite will be held
and a true light encircle
our planet's destiny
transforming the nightmare of time
into a new Day's ray.

Europe, 24 October 2000

Dear Mary Magdalene

Some people say they are on their way to the graveyard,
but I say I am on my way to the resurrection and a time
when life is not a burden any more. Of course I know the
world has been put off balance but you know that this
time is a miracle-worker and everything will be changed
utterly.

My presence has not always been easy in your absence.
In my dreams I have been able to see your eyes, the joy in
these eyes... Yes, you are a real harbinger of joy and I
must now and then call up your presence, your singing
voice in the desert, your arms, your whole body, and your
morning smile... At this very moment I know you are real
and I can feel the air around you. It is not spring, but a
spring wind is here and perhaps you are riding a bike or
walking in some street in this city (Stockholm) where a

lot of people are speculating on the Stock Exchange... In the papers you can read about winners and losers.

Autumn rain and autumn darkness and sometimes the sun. You are a flute-player; you can drum, dance, sing... and when you meet people at a café (the Café Albert?) you can tell them the truth: we are not yet born but on the horizon there is a promising light. Every breath is of importance, every thought...

The old millennium has had its say; your time is dawning. I bid you welcome... Natasha, Isis, Hathor, Inanna, Shanti, the Black Madonna, the Goddess of the Gospels, whoever you may be, you are welcome to join me and this mysterious creation play. Have I by now entered your imagination? Can you see me? This year – the year 2000 – is silent. But soon 2001... will speak.

PS. Egypt's Eastern Desert, 5 February 2001. The desert and the Red Sea, and the Sun Ra... I wish you were here, and perhaps you are – in your thoughts...?... The temples and the Nile are waiting. What are you up to? – Do you write? Or do you ride a wild horse on the steppe? – In a dream I saw our world to come, clear, brilliant, sharply outlined, like a city in a tale you can read in the world's most magic book.

In a dream some years ago I saw our new horizon and heard the words:

A New Child will be born.
The Sun is in his mind:
The Rising of the Spiritual Sun.

Texts for Shanti and Mary Magdalene

We are sleeping in a body that is the *Last Night of the Body*. Our time is a miracle adventure – not yet revealed.

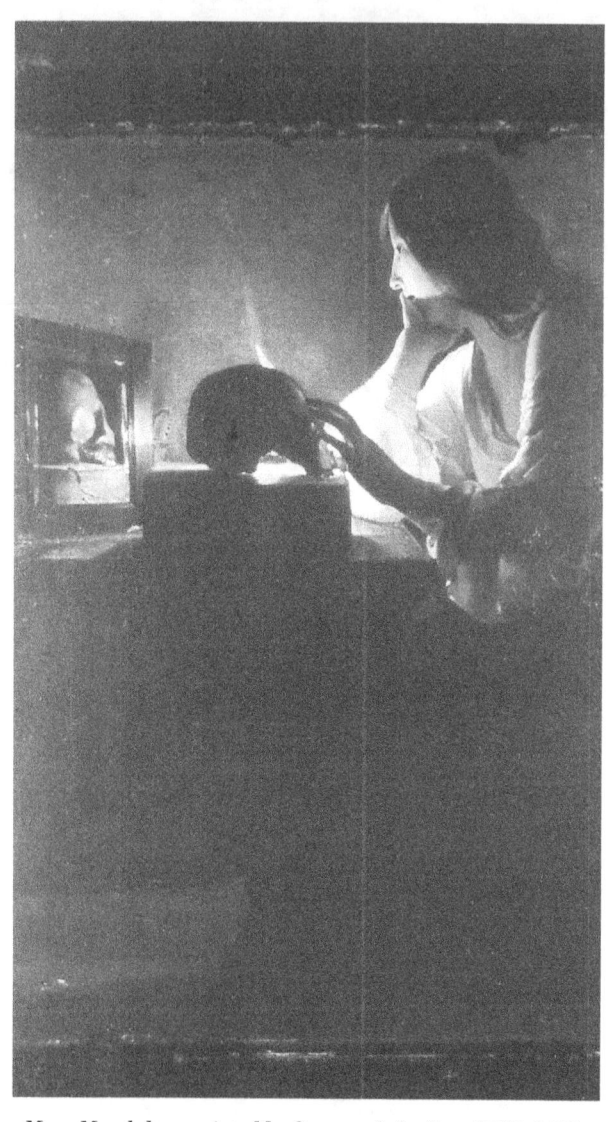

Mary Magdalene painted by Georges de La Tour (1593-1652).
The National Gallery of Art, Washington.

Words to Hans Christian

You remember Hans Christian Ostrø*. Before he left
for India I said to him:
  "The future man will have a very high sensitivity. He
will move like an angel in the room and communicate
through his light... Yes, you can – as you know –
communicate with your light, and when you start to
communicate through the language of light, the words will
become a secondary communication."

(January 1995)

*See letters: 21 August 1995 and 7 March 1998. Many articles
mentioning Hans Christian – actor, poet, and dancer – were published
in the year 1995 all over the world.

Who Are You?
(At a Tailor's Shop in Bangkok)

"Where do you come from? Where were you born?"
   "I live in this country."
   "Yes, but which is your home country?"
   "I belong to all countries. The planet. The Universe."
   "Yes, of course; but I mean: Where were you born?
Which country?"
   "I am originally from the sun. I am a solar incarnation
now working here with my work in progress. I am a
poet, a dramatist, an artist. I am a creative writer. It
means you create a new life each day. You do not repeat.
You make all things new."
   "But you must have a home."
   "I've already told you. The Universe. It's enough for
me."
   "Yes. But your native country?"

Etcetera.

(April 1997)

Some Impressions from India, April 1998

India is a democracy where new information technology is flourishing, but India is also a holy continent that is trying to forget about its holiness. It is a banyan tree full of singing birds and a meditative monkey sitting on a balcony half past six, just before sunrise in Har(i)dwar (God's Gate). It is white-clad people greeting the Easter sunrise and remembering the resurrection of Jesus Christ. It is a country killing the air by using engines from the West and fuel from the Arabian world; it is obtrusive beggars and rich businessmen, kindness and generosity... strong and weak authority, great poetry and art...

Holy Ganga is still there, full of power at the Gate of God, where orange-clad sadhus moved in ecstasy during the Khumb(a) Mela 1998 – after having taken dips in the eternity-giving water.

Some politicians are trying to rule people governed by a spirit that they may not be able to understand. Here and everywhere... Maybe the future India, the goddess India, has a gift for mankind if she takes care of her true spirit within herself and opens her mind to a reality where the individual soul can develop in freedom and peace in collaboration with the non-destructive powers of nature – the powers that don't pollute man's environment. But how many can today – without scruples – worship (as Rabindranath Tagore says in his poem *New Birth*) God in Man?

A Vision of the Future

I listen to my heartbeats and the heartbeats of the world.
A voice says: "Humanity is now a peaceful unity. Dis-
trust, distortion, distress, disunion... don't exist any more.
Even diseases belong to the past." – I hear the voices of
the past night and the voices of a new morning... All blind
ages are gone. The Solar Temple – *Intihuasi* (Coricancha)
in Cuzco – is once more the Golden Place of the Sun.

(Cuzco, Peru, 14 June 1999)

At an Airport in Europe, 12 August 1999

Inspector (I)
Passenger (P)

I: We must have your permission to search you – from head to foot.
P: And if I don't consent?
I: Then you have to stay.
P: I have to go to Paris. But if I stay: what am I to do with my tickets?
I: Then you have to consent.
P: Consent to what? To a disgusting, humiliating search? I am not a criminal. I am a transit passenger on my way to Paris. In Edinburgh an hour ago they where humane. I could pass through their inspection without being searched. Isn't that enough?
I: Well, if you don't consent...
P: But why?
I: We have our laws, our obligations. We have to do this to protect all passengers.
P: Yes, I can understand. But you are not the Gestapo, are you?
I: We have our laws. It's nothing we can do about it.
P: So then you have to pass through a public humiliation that I don't like – because of your laws?
I: Well, that's the law.
P: And you are the law and I the chosen victim?
I: No, I just obey.
P: Then, who is the law? I don't want to give my permission. But I cannot stay in England, and I don't want to give up my ticket to Paris. What kind of freedom is this? I am a European tourist, not a criminal. I'm passing through a European nation, and I don't have

167

time to go by train to Paris where I will see friends and give a poetry reading.

I: You have your free will to do what you like.

P: To force a tourist to give somebody permission to paw him – is that humane? Isn't it rather an undue encroachment?

I: If you don't like it you will have to stay.

P: I wonder: What kind of freedom do you have in this society? Is there any freedom of thought? of creative expression? of body integrity? I'm the owner of my own body. Or am I not?

I: Well, if you don't consent...

P: I know you are an obedient inspector, a good servant, but I don't want to...

I: We have the police.

P: Yes, you have the power. The outer power. But what about the inner? I know I must obey because I must be in Paris today. – I am a writer, a yogi, and not an insensitive robot. Let your henchman do what he has to do. For you it might be a routine check-up. But I cannot just wash my hands of it as you do.

PS.

Ora pro nobis, ora pro nobis...

Once Jeanne d'Arc (Joan of Arc) said:

"J'ai peur. Où est la vérité?"

Where is the truth (la vérité) today? In a police station? in the court? at the theatre?

Or perhaps nowhere?

To be afraid – like Jeanne – is a feeling anybody can understand – especially those who have confronted people with a Gestapo-mentality. Or at least: an inhumanity nobody would expect in a highly civilized country in Europe.

Paris and Saint-Clair-sur-Epte, August 1999

On 13 August 1999 I was introduced to a writer at the bookshop Shakespeare and Company in Paris. He was from Italy and spoke English fluently. I asked:

"Are you a poet?"

He said:

"Ah well, I just write poetry when I feel depressed and when I am ill."

I answered:

"I understand. I know. I have at least once written poetry during a high fever."

Then I thought: But what is poetry? Now and then you have to write in order to survive. Not economically but mentally and in every sense. Some people write poetry when they are ill, or are in love. Some don't write at all. They are being written. The poetry is always there. It's the true reality in the history of mankind. If you have a third ear you just have to listen and you can hear it speaking to you from an eternal source without end.

☆

I came to Paris from Normandie where I visited the St Clair Castle (begun in the tenth century) and the holy well at Saint-Clair-sur-Epte and was told that the well became holy after the beheading of the hermit St Clair in the ninth century. William de Saint Clair, the builder of Rosslyn Chapel close to Edinburgh, possibly knew that his name derived from this hermit and had really many reasons to defend the Holy Light. The legend tells that the hermit took his head in his hands and brought it to the well and then to a place where the church now stands. Every year – on 17 July – they celebrate this miracle.

They walk in procession and light a huge fire and hund-
reds of candles on the meadow close to the holy well.

Xmas Time

Time: Christmas Day 1999. *Place*: A lookout on a hill near Lake Petén Itzá, Guatemala.

I was invited to come up to the roof, the highest look-out-place of the futuristic-looking back-packer-*posada* Mirador del Duende. And there they sat, two men, looking at the lake, the water, the clear blue sky, the rainforest. They talked about the Universe, the Inverse the Multiverse... the Children of Time, the cycles...

I had given them some information on my book *Time Plays*. I greeted them with a peace greeting, hands together, like they do in India when they say: "Namasté".

I said: "La Paz sea con vosotros." (Peace be unto you.)

They knew only a few English words.

I was dressed in white among white futuristic buildings with openings suggestive of Mayan architecture. The blue... Or rather: the almost white sky. The sun shone. A cock was heard and the traffic on the road to Tikal; and far away a radio song from a Maya hut: "Silent Night, Holy Night." It was in the afternoon, half an hour before sunset. A silence reigned in the heavens – a silence you could feel if you didn't stir and listened. No petrol fume, no noise...

Suddenly nobody talked. But all listened... So what could you expect:

"La Paz sea con vosotros."

Change of Millennium – Mexico and Guatemala

Dream on a bus to Chetumal: Browsing the pages of the Universe, the Inverse, the inverse universe. Skimming through the pages of the book *Cosmos*, losing the attention, missing some pages here and there... And what happened then? Did a message arrive that I didn't get? a crown of light I never saw?

I am now writing in the midday heat at Chetumal, Southern Mexico:

> Arrival, departure, arrival, departure...
> A slot machine...
> Is this life a slot machine?
> Please, proceed to Gate number Nine!
> "What the hail?"
> The sun rose,
> The wind laughed,
> The moon sang...
> We are disciples and masters
> In a universe university...
> The universe university is the new school...
> *Waves, waves, waves...*

Who is creating music of the world? (*a dream sentence*)

☆

Have you ever listened to the voices of the engines? They must feel sick – all of them... Whining and groaning and mourning and wailing. – Go back to the moment of truth before any civilization began!

Swedish is a tongue, English... Can I say something in Swedish? To whom?

Now staying at the Hotel Posada del Angel... Has anybody arrived? Any body? Outside: tropical downpour.

Somebody asked me in Spanish: "Do you have any religion?" I answered: "No." And then I said: "Or perhaps: El universo en total" (the universe as a totality).

A couple of days ago I was reading a menu at the "Coffee Press" (a café at Playa del Carmen): "*Om*: High-grown Darjeeling tea and the mumbled chantings of a certified tea shaman."

☆

Drums. Dance. The plazas and the pyramids are there in the jungle. But no drums and no dancing. Tourists are climbing and walking around and trying to understand what all this is about. I am trying to find a language, dreaming of drums in a forest, a Tikal ruin music. – Where are the sacred dancers? Where is the woman I saw in my dream, a human being with a natural openness, softness, and a necklace that rattled like waves on a seashore?

I can hear the waves of Lake Petén Itzá. It's noon. I remember the birds and the animals (the howlers, the macaws, the toucans, the montezuma birds, the spider monkeys, and the long-nosed small friendly furry animals) in the jungle of Tikal. I also recall the full moon at night over the Giant Jaguar Pyramid and the pyramid of *El Mundo Perdido* (The Lost World).

It's soon the end of a whole millennium. We are living in the Endgame. In the beginning is my end, or if possible: in the end is my beginning. Now the time of the new sun is here, the golden Horus is entering the new stage.

A bird zings across the white day sky... and I've felt the unrest in the human life, the common modern civilized life without deeper meaning... You buy and sell and run...

173

climb the pyramids in no time, run too much and hurt yourself.

How many words do you need in order to survive, to be accepted, to earn a living...?...

Night, full moon. Hardly a breath can be heard in the jungle.

I told a friend, Gustavo from Toluca in Mexico: "This could be a dream world, a world that many people have felt hides a certain secret, a special secret, a cosmos key... a world where a high-pitched music once moved the stones and filled the heart with peace."

This was at Tikal, and I asked myself: *What have I done during the past dark era?* – A struggle for survival? Yes. A quest for a stage for all my plays, for co-actors, for money needed in the art production, for a voice I now know, a voice and soul I call Inanna, and she is, when I write these lines, somewhere on the west coast of Mexico – the Land of the Dead according to the ancient myth.

Have I succeeded in my tries to communicate? No. I've been living on four continents during the seventies, eighties and nineties... And of course I have friends. I even know a few who have read some of my written and published works.

And still...?...

Yes, I felt at home in Tikal under the sun, under the full moon... And I love the sounds of the jungle, the birds in the World Tree, the furry animals: my long-nosed friends.

I feel my play, *The Last Night of the Body*, ought to be staged in a sacred plaza in Tikal or Uxmal. – *The Last Night of the Body*: my most genuine message for a future mankind.

Booming roads, petrol stench.

Today – 23 December 1999 – it is exactly 13 years before the end of the Mayan Great Cycle (13 *Baktuns*) that started on 11 August 3114 B.C. according to some authorities.

174

In my beginning is my end, in my end my beginning.

I must say that I once had a mother tongue. I don't have it any more. And yet I have to express myself in a tongue. In Tikal – beside the Giant Jaguar Pyramid – I used a wind instrument (a very small one) that created the earth tone all over the nearby plazas and inaugurated a new era's day.

Well, I must admit that I really like the small furry animals of the Tikal jungle. They are, as I have already said, long-nosed and always very busy looking for food among the leaves and the grass on the ground. Their long noses search and search, and they have got accustomed to people: back-packers, ordinary tourists, and pyramid sleepers looking for a final revelation that would explain why we are here on this planet where life is explored by the humans but has never been really understood.

It's a new day. It's almost noon. It's Christmas Day. I write these words in my bungalow near the lake, Lago Petén Itzá, in Guatemala. Some birds are chirping. An insect is buzzing. A friend of mine has hurt her leg. The clouds are gathering over the lake. Rain has been falling now and then during the last few days.

A voice in space says: "What was this life? A VISA card lost in an ATM (a cash dispenser) in Santa Elena, Guatemala, on Christmas Eve? You lose a card and cannot pay your room, your food, your laundry, your life. What was this life? this *Mundo Perdido**?"

Faces and stones, stelaes smashed to pieces, no body no more, no tongue, but still... I don't even want to be understood. And still they try, the experts... And naturally I understand: the decomposition, the civilized muck, the devil's work.

---

*El Mundo Perdido (the Lost World) is a complex (in Tikal) of 38 structures with a pyramid in its midst. The impressive Mayan city called Tikal was abandoned more than a thousand years ago.

The old Maya world is a riddle – as much a riddle as the works of Beckett. Samuel Beckett once wrote to me in a letter: "Herewith my latest gasp" – meaning his book *Assez* (Enough) which he sent me. I haven't as yet sent this letter to Lois More Overbeck, Emory University (The Correspondence of Samuel Beckett), Atlanta, USA. But perhaps I ought to...?...

I can now realize that Beckett was a really living human being, exceptional in the laureated field of art.

Still. Assez. Enough. – The jostling, the lack of sensitivity, men who woggle and wobble and spit... and our glorified, roaring, stinking Faust civilization – that one day will be a tale told by the survivors – if there are any... Or...?...

Words said to somebody while I was overlooking Lake Petén Itzá: "This is Xmas 1999, but time is an ocean that is a veil. The timeless being is a body without limbs that we shall understand when the earth begins a new breathing."

It is Xmas, and I recall that the ATM swallowed my VISA card at Santa Elena, a somewhat dilapidated town where a drunkard was the kindest man when I needed help. He knocked at the door of the Banco Industrial that had swallowed my card. But it was Christmas Eve and nobody opened.

So here I am – without card, without money, and almost without a mother tongue – in a world ruled by money.

☆

Thinking of some words in Beckett's *Krapp's Last Tape*: "Seventeen copies sold... Getting known. [---] The earth might be uninhabited." – Well, I'm not there yet: "Seventeen copies". – Never mind... One day...

Banks and cranks, a cranky world... What in creation is all this about?

My long-nosed friend, Tikal, Guatemala.

The Giant Jaguar Pyramid, Tikal ("The Place of the Voices").

The Giant Jaguar Pyramid in Tikal is real. Not the shrieking cars...

Now drinking a cup of chocolate at a restaurant beside Lake Petén Itzá. The old millennium, the old dark chill, is breathing its last... Children are playing in the quiet streets of Flores looking at pictures of the past Maya gods who are tales and myths and in the near future possibly something more than that.

If people could preserve the rainforest there would be plenty of work for the new gods, and the new plays on the plazas between the pyramids (for instance at Tikal), new ritual dramas, like my play *The Last Night of the Body,* could be performed.

My time has been a time full of invocations: "Save me from the civilized infernos, the Funeral's last gaps, the endgame's final steps..." – I'm sometimes praying like little Gerard, Jack Kerouac's brother, used to pray (see Kerouac's book *Visions of Gerard*).

When water and air and solar power are the fuels and the power everywhere, you could say: *This world is a paradise.* – And what will happen to the money that has gone astray in the wrong pockets and the nuclear waste that is poisoning the earth?

I can see the clear lakes and the wise forest people (not the nuclear people). The new millennium will not agree to any dark creation. We are all here in this creation mystery play, in this time play when Time plays.

I wish I could bring an action against all war nations for libel. A woebegun civilized world makes me seasick, saltsick... I've squandered too much time in its lap. It's a lugubrious world full of bad taste. I know people try to spruce up as well as they can. But they are lost... What they create is a thousand "yeses" and "that's rights" and "that's wrongs" as Jack Kerouac and other geniuses have realized.

The old time is full of misbeliefs, mischiefs, and mis-behaviour. But my dream time is consoling.

179

In a dream I came into a huge palace, where I couldn't find my way out. I asked a guardian and was told that I could choose between 22 exits.

Which one should I choose?

People, time, vehicles... zipped by... And finally I saw the opening where I'd never expected an opening.

The roof had been opened. The light of the sky was everywhere!

☆

No, I cannot say I ever lived, but I must say I have felt the presence of real life on many occasions, for instance at a bus station in India where I saw a spark of a life from a dream world almost forgotten and beyond measure.

☆

Words said in a dream: "Some of my plays are transitional time plays translated from my past existences."

(December 1999 – January 2000)

Dialogue

"Where are you from?"
  "I am from nowhere."
  "Norway?"
  "No. I said Nowhere."
  "But you must be coming from somewhere."
  "No, but I might go somewhere. I am not coming. I am here."
  "Here? But you said you came from..."
  "... Nowhere."
  "And you are going to...?"
  "Any place, any time, any life... where I can live in peace and be respected for what I am: a Nowhere man going to Anywhere."
  "How strange you are."
  "No, not at all. Everybody in this Somewhere is coming from Nowhere."

(Playa del Carmen, Mexico, 2000)

At a Gallery in Cancún

"Who are you?"

(*No answer.*)

"I know you write in English. But are you English?"

"No, but I listen to the Angels, and they speak to me in English."

"Then you are a sensitive man and not an insensitive crime writer?"

"Insensitivity is in my eyes not a mark of crime, but isn't it at least a mark of disease?"

"Have you never wanted to be a criminal?"

"No, I am neither a cracksman nor a blasphemer. I will not crack a crib. But I have been living beyond my means, and I cannot esteem people that go smack like a rhinoceros."

"Then who are you?"

"Time will tell. And who are you?"

(Yucatán, Mexico, in the year 2000)

An Odd Coincidence in Cancún

A vaulted white bridge across a Venice-like canal. I walked together with a kind but somewhat confused man who looked for a true track in this life-jungle and now almost believed in a religion that had outplayed its role in the history of man. This man – who had not yet been able to discover the real reality of the outer and the inner sun – introduced me to a young "lion-man", who took care of several lions. He had within himself a natural subtlety you can find only in the depth of a primeval forest or on a smooth river in the midst of a jungle untouched by civilized man. Probably the lions had taught him to move and behave in a way that respected the spaces between one being and another. He didn't have to dive into the darkness of all the religious seas or lose himself in any superstition. He knew how to be here and now and forever – in the poetry, in the poem, in the very centre of Creation.

Where Are You?

Where are you
In this empty room without end?
I must speak to somebody,
but I can hear nobody...

What can we do in a world
full of street noise and head noise?
Fight for survival everywhere. Why?
Why fight? Fight against death, fight
against life... And the world is asleep,
a deep sleep no doubt, or is it on the point
of awakening?

To stand on Earth, to cry for salvation,
or go back in history, meet Antonello
da Messina and see if there is a hidden
message behind all these time curtains...

Rubbish everywhere but also a glimmer
of true reality, of gold mornings, of
a truth that I imagine Antonello, the painter, knew...

But I am not sure. A secret hidden in
the fifteenth century? I wonder.

(Spring 1997)

A New Breathing

Wound in linen... No.
Now living – in a
Silent room in a desert
Where songs are heard,
Songs filling the air
And making my breathing easier...

The Kingdom of Ashes
Has lost its power.
A new Kingdom is rising out of the ashes.
A new breathing is born.

Time has shifted.
Our future is our past.
Our past our future.

I speak from the beginning of time;
I am Time's prisoner no more...

(India 1998)

The Son of the Dust

(For Jim)

The son of the dust,
the dust in the sun,
the sun dust... the sun
of the dust... in a Pushkar street...

A solar smile in the dust,
a son of man in this time,
at Pushkar, a small town
by a holy lake... in India...

A man without legs
smiling like a sun, a sun man,
in the heat, in the sun,
in the shade, in a dusty street,
almost in the realm of shades...

a solar dust man
in a holy temple town, a human being
full of a miraculous joy
whose source is beyond
common sense, common words,
common worlds...

(1998)

A Magic Room

In a dream I saw:
A magic seat, a throne in a throne room,
Two cheetas or two leopards,
One on each side of the throne,
A magnetic power field all around,
A kingdom where everything is holy,
The trees, the drum, a woman's hand...

Her fingers, her gait, like an angel,
Like a black cat, completely natural,
A holy secret in man's nature, the wisdom
Of the soul, of a true presence with a language
Beyond words... gliding through a forest of
Majestic pillars, trunks, crowns, flowers...
And lakes...

The woman's voice said:

"We have seen the full moon of the First World.
We have seen the full moon of the Second...
Now the Third World must be created,
The world of the sunrise...
Yes, Life itself can now start
To play and show its real uplifting force
Within man's nature... and beyond Time's source..."

(Lanzarote, at the end of December 1998)

The Day of Destiny

Close to Notre-Dame,
A pleasantly warm evening,
13 August 1999,
The Day of Destiny...
Sitting in front of a whole book-world:
Shakespeare and Company.

Time has run out,
And time is here...
People are moving
In the darkness after sunset:
Silent steps, silent breath,
Voices, cars; no moon...

Who is praying in this night?
Who is waiting round the corner?
Who is looking for a true story?

The Story is always somewhere else.
It has never started.
It will never begin.
Our life is already gone
And still an eternity
We have never met...

We hear noise, a voice, voices...
How much do we understand?
Time has run out.
People are moving in the darkness...

The Spirit of the Creative Word

Shut your eyes and ears: What do you hear?
A whole world is speaking.
Listen and you can hear:
The spirit of the creative word is here
Changing Time's face.

(Paris, 19 August 1999)

Caye Caulker, Belize.

Caye Caulker, January 2000

I

I am a walker
On Caye Caulker,
I walk in the sand
On the sandy roads
And listen to the silent vehicles
Remembering the name of a shop:
"Likkle bit a dis & likkle bit a dat",
Seeing the sun rise,
Seeing the sun set,
Listening to the drunkards
Who have been up all night,
Having hardly any voice left
When they say: "Good morning"
To the passers-by...
Listening to the strange birds
And the roosters
And the wind
And the storm, and the rain, and
The strong wind through the windows...
And the lightning...
And the sky...
And the rainbow,
The hopeful sign...
And remembering a man
Who sat watching the cloud play
On the sea horizon, the changing colours of sunset:
"Look! The colours are changing every five
        seconds!"

II

Come and see
The Caribbean Sea
In the evening sun,
Come, come...

It's blue and green
And the rain comes and goes...
Palm leaves rattle in the wind.
A pelican dives
And a racoon is walking along the sandy road
Between pink, yellow, and blue houses...
Far away, near the horizon
You can see the white coral reef
And a red ship with a white cloud behind it.

Come, come and see
The Caribbean Sea
And listen to the wind,
Faraway voices
And rattling palm leaves...

III

Keep still,
Do not stir,
Be like Holy Week,
Calm down,
Keep your arms still,
Stand still, listen:
Suddenly a hush comes over the room,
You hear the silence. And then:
A wind through the windows
And the waves that lap the shore...

The day is soon gone,
The sky plays...
The birds are playing...
The will of the new space gods say:
Sky, earth, water, the theatre...
The play, the roots, the trunk, the crown,
The healing sound:
Drums, slow and quick beats,
Like the forest leaves...
The drummers of the forest are beating their drums,
A polyrhythmic sound
On the earth,
A virgin ground...
And no noxious fume
In this sacred room...

IV

I say: "Great is the Day."
But I know of course that I've been
Cut and bruised...
Still nobody has stolen my vision of
A solar ship's coast where my senses
And body are healed and the future
Of man revealed...

And there I can see you again, lady of morning,
Of light and peace... lady of silences
And delight...

That gives me release and makes me forget
The suicidal pavements of the world,
The dungeons, the sharp edges, the fidgets,
The bars, the cars, the wrong energy...

The oil industry hell gone, not even as strong
As a weak memory now when I've regained
My balance and can dance in freedom again

On the coast where you are, under a free sky,
Under the stars... under the moon and the sun...

Saying: "Great is the Day." Yes, great
Is our day and our morning's sun.

Tongue Mother

my tongue is my mother
but I don't have any mother tongue any more
and no tongue mother
I have to create a new tongue
that can be my real mother
more than any other mother tongues
a real tongue mother
containing all tongues

The End of the Waste Land

No, no crucifixion and no fire... You say:
"Thanks, I've got enough..."
Crucified and burnt at the stake again and again
since time immemorial...
And always, centuries after centuries:
a quest for the truth; your search for a man,
the Man, is still going on –
the True Man, hidden in the future,
or maybe the past.

Readers of the Gospels, readers of
the future, lost souls on beaches, in cities,
what do you see?
Of course: birds with forked tails,
fishermen, drummers in the night,
passers-by... men shaken to the core...

Burning, burning, burning... you see
the waste vast land
and a war within everybody...
Everywhere the battle of the soul
within a body nobody knows
and everybody mistreats
until the Man, the true human being,
finally sees and is
the key, the breath,
the interspaces
outside time's crucifixion history.

The real truth might be
a writing in water or air,
unattainable and ethereal...

But the Search, the Quest, goes on...
And at the end of the time of crucifixion
the birds are talking in the air;
the heirs of truth are entering the stage
and a feeling of peace
after war, fire, and waste
are filling the space
and the souls of the holy waters.

(Caye Caulker, Belize, January 2000)

Far from a Prosaic Proposal

"Why don't we marry on a Hawaiian beach?"

"Who has said that we are going to marry?"

"The angels, I suppose."

"And what did they say?"

"That the destiny of mankind wants our cooperation."

"That's crazy. You are crazy..."

"Yes, I speak the truth. And all true relatives will be invited: the stars, the song-birds, the heavenly solar people, etcetera."

"So that's your folks?"

"Yea, you damn right, that's my buddies."

"Who are you by the way?"

"A rope walker, a hidden secret, a gone purgation and a revelation beyond all nightmare. I don't have a hide like a rhinoceros, and I am no Tarzan, but still..."

"Hawaii, you said? A hieros gamos on a Hawaiian beach or...?..."

"Anywhere would do, now when the Son of Man and his Bride are entering the stage, now when the sun in man and the moon in man will meet so that a true peace finally can be established and a more humane world can be created..."

"You mean a new creation?"

"Yes."

And the Bride Said

And the Bride said:
"The right time is here...
You're turning...
I am.
We are all changed utterly.
And in the Shrine
deep in our mind
we shall find
a new life growing
in the old tree."

Time Space Music

The eternal moment
In a never-ending time spirit
Is
The everlasting
Saviour's Time Space Music
In time's turnstile.
Back through God's ages eternally
The answer of the Riddle
Of Creation
Is never found.
But signs in time can guide you.

(3 August 2000)

She Is Here

In a dream I told a man in a medieval town: "I shall go to the King and tell him who I am." – But what should I tell the King? – Should I say: "I've lived in a country at the end of the world, at the end of Time... I am half a stranger, half a citizen of the world. Some people know my name, but do they know me? Do they know the moment of truth on a stage full of trash? Who is looking for a meaning in this dark labyrinth?... Now I remember: She told me: 'Silence! the Goddess speaks.' – Does she know who I am, will she be able to utter the right words and give me back my true role in a theatre where people have lost their common sense and can see nothing but disaster?... Maybe she has the answer to the riddle I am, maybe she is the answer... being here on this stage... being a human... a being... in a body, soul and body and spirit in the mist, on the road, in the street, in the sun... But who knows? Am I? And where is she now?"

Shall I meet the King? Will he say:

"The Stranger, the Witness, the Critic is here together with the Virgin-Bride, the Goddess. *Please preserve respectful distance*, as a poet once said... Silence! the Goddess speaks in the silence. Silence! the Stranger speaks..."...

I can see how the Goddess, thinking she has met a lesser king and not her true King, gets into a rage. Flashes of lightning in the sky. Her words are written in the firmament.

And what will happen when the Stranger addresses the Goddess? I listen and can hear his voice:

"Your words are full of wrath; you have vented your anger on (what you call) 'a lesser king'... Can I say, I am not only a voice or a dream or a non-existent being in this

Universe where your presence has been longed-for since time immemorial...?... Who is my mother? my sisters and brothers? my Beloved?... Do you know more about me than I do? I'm not sure. But I know you agree when I say: the Sacred Wedding or Marriage is of utter importance in a time when 'the Son of man shall send forth his angels'... And if – as you say – your so-called lesser king is an offender against the Goddess, I really hope he will be pardoned... Is there a reason behind it all, some higher will that this accused king has disregarded?... Is there anybody who can punish him, expel him from the Kingdom of Life?... I cannot answer that question. I don't know if I have any power at all. But when I listen to the inner voices of this universe I can hear the voices of the children of the resurrection. Are they my kin?... Yes, I believe they are. And I know: to be a human being is not an easy task. You have to learn and suffer many things. The Master (or rather his angels) once said: 'Why seek ye the living among the dead?' – Have you ever understood that sentence?... Once they said about the Master: 'He is not here, but is risen.' ... But you are here. I am now totally convinced... *Peace be unto you*, Goddess of Heaven and Earth. The Holy Spirit Inspiration will guide us. And I can hear your song in this immense forest where I've doubted your existence. Now I can see an end to all trials, darkness, desert life... I am thirsty, I must drink, I want to survive. The Quest has finally brought me home – to the TIME-SPACE where you are..."

Yes, this is a dream... and yet: *She is here, He... the King...* and everybody knows everybody else in a dream world where everybody takes part in the unfinished and forever ongoing story of the Creation.

(2001...)

202

Eastern Desert, February 2001

People ask: "From where are you? Where do you come from? Which is your native country?"

The Stranger answers: "I am coming from a country beyond all nations and borders. Nations have always disturbed my sense of universal harmony. And by the way: Who are you, in time's eternal flow? Where have you landed? been seen, been spoken to?"

The spirit of the place where the Stranger had landed (in Egypt) said to him:

"A world, a surge of words...
Reverse the world, the words, the wounded time,
Reverse the sunless mind...

Blessed be our soul
Now and forever.
Amen.

Reverse the fear, the years,
The experience of lost peace, lost love,
Lost fights, nights, and daily dearth.
Reverse the Universe, release, give birth..."

☆

Here in the desert I was a stranger, and yet no stranger. I saw a shadow, then another shadow, then a third... And finally the truth: the world was as if transfigured by a light beyond description, your presence at last – a reality.

A desert spirit in Egypt's Eastern Desert.

A Letter to the Reader

Yes, you are right, Shanti is a person who is a real person, and most of the letters have been written to her. Only a few have other recipients, e.g. letters to a Goddess and a Space Sister and Solar Sister who could also be called Shanti. *Shanti* is a Sanskrit word for peace, welfare, prosperity, good fortune... a common female name in India. It is peace mankind has been unable to create so far, the peace of body, soul, and mind.

Can you see these letters as steps towards this goal? In them you can find impressions from four continents during a time when we passed from one millennium to another. At last the time of the Son, the crucified Master of the past time, is no more. And Mary Magdalene – MM, the year 2000 – enters the stage. Now the Bride can meet the Bridegroom. The end and rebeginning is at hand.

Once – in the year of 1995 – I said to an audience words that could be of some significance to a reader of this book: "Shut your eyes and imagine that you are somewhere in a dark space in the universe. Your mind is blank, completely blank. And all of a sudden you discover a point, a bright point, maybe the sun... Try to identify yourself with this point, see it in front of you, don't lose it, make it stand still, don't let it pass away... If possible: be one with it. – Open your eyes: it's still there within you or in front of you, isn't it?... Now your mind can function as a good transmitter and a good receiver. You are really here. You are a sighted person, you can read between the lines and understand."

The text "The Day of Destiny" (see p. 188 and p. 136) was first read during my poetry reading at the bookshop Shakespeare and Company in Paris, 19 August 1999.

205

I had been invited by Shakespeare and Company to read from my new book *Time Plays*, and in my reading I included "The Day of Destiny", an entry in my diary, written some days earlier. The text "Junction at Sunrise" from *Time Plays* concluded the reading.

The poem "The Son of the Dust" (page 186) was written after a conversation over the phone with James Knowlson, author of e.g. *Damned to Fame. The Life of Samuel Beckett*. We talked about Beckett's theatre and my India experiences in 1998, when I met a beggar who reminded me of a character in a Beckett play.

Art Distribution (A.D.), mentioned in a letter written in December 1994, is a small non-profit cultural foundation that has been active in the fields of art (literature, theatre, dance, music, etc.) during several decades. Its work is aiming at a better environment and a possibility of a free outlet for different kinds of artistic creativity. Its most important project is called Theatre Europe – not only meant to be a theatre but also a free cultural university open to creative impulses from all parts of the world.

Europe in April 2002

Postscript. Costa de la Luz 2003

The first edition of this book was very limited (only 36 copies). The second edition is also very limited, but non-numbered. When will a non-limited edition appear? I don't know yet.

Time is playing. The peace people are very active, and there is hope in this light on Costa de la Luz (The Coast of Light).

On 13 September 2002, when I was staying on the island of Bonaire in the South Caribbean, I wrote:
" 'Au commencement: le Logos, le Logos est vers Dieu, le Logos est Dieu' (the initial words in the translation of the Gospel according to St. John by Jean-Yves Leloup).

"Does this mean that the Logos (the divine and creative Word, the human reason, and God's revelation in the divine creation) is meant to be directed towards a goal we can call God?

"If we look upon God as all human spiritual inheritance and endeavour, we could say that all humanity is heading for this goal in the spirit. Perhaps this was the intention of the original Creator, who in the beginning uttered the Word of Light and at the end of creation will bring humanity back to its own source, the original Light World (Light Word)?

"Some people say the gods and goddesses known to the ancient cultures are again in touch with the earth and its human beings, and many men and women feel the importance of a rebirth of a ritual mentioned in *Letters to Shanti*, the *hieros gamos* rite, that probably, at the beginning of time, gave the inspiration that created what we call the Garden of Eden."

Shanti Words after 2012

"Sandhyas! Sandhyas! Sandhyas! Calling all downs. Calling all downs to dayne. Array! Surrection" are words, world words, in James Joyce's Finnegans Wake. The end of the old world is gone. The old sun, the old time, has done its work. The new sun is rising. The new vehicles of the Word have descended to the stage of manifestation.

Every year is a Shanti year. The year 2000, 2013, 2016, 3000 ... What will be is. What is will be.

Letters to Shanti was first published at the beginning of the new millennium in two very limited art editions. This new edition has no limits but the limits of the readers.

T.S. Eliot's poem *The Waste Land* ends with the words "Shantih shantih shantih", and the word Shanti(h) means peace beyond all understanding. The peace on earth we have seen until now has been a limited peace and not a peace beyond understanding. Even the culture of at least the Western world has lacked both peace and understanding.

About 200 years ago the poet William Blake once wrote:

"Art degraded, Imagination Denied, War Governs the Nations! Rouse Up, O Young Men of the New Age!"

Yes, William Blake is talking about the new age, an age when science and art will blend together and be the source of all creative work. But will humanity succeed in using the inspiration and creative ability on a peaceful artistic level?

Everybody wants to earn money: publishers, authors, readers, reviewers ... On the outskirts of this "semitary of Somnionia" (Joyce) there may be a few living spirits.

Are they able to ignite a new fire, to kindle a new era, where "Heliotropolis, the castellated, the enchanting" (see Joyce's *Finnegans Wake*) will be the spiritual capital of the world?

Many human beings may think they have the solution to all problems, and too many are afraid of themselves and of others. Many societies are hostile towards poetic creativity, children's playfulness, and the true comforting feminine carefulness.

You are working hard. You are paying your taxes. You are trying to survive, learning to breathe, learning to dance, voting, fighting, acting, reacting, repressing, abusing, refusing ... The whole earth itself is being raped by its mighty rulers. The so called religions are sometimes a disaster, and weapons are being used against innocent people.

"I am but two days old" are words by William Blake in his book *Songs of Innocence and of Experience*. Yes, I am but two days old, and I will not become older. The universe is to me a university and a universal playground. All cultures have their gold mines, and the true gold may be found in people who can see "a heaven in a wild flower" (Blake).

No, I am not dreaming about people's outstanding successes in life. My life has been an adventurous challenge and it still is. And I am addressing you who never give up hope of a happy survival in this universe beyond all universities. No, I have not passed any useful exams and will probably never do. But like the Italian renaissance philosopher Giordano Bruno, I am passing through all universes. And I can see this little earth as it is: a threatend pearl of a life we have not as yet understood.

Load your camera, but not your gun! Be aware of your word and the tone of your voice, the power in your thought and the life in your breath. If you want to be a judge, then judge yourself first of all. This is a good starting-point, but it is not the key that opens all doors.

Where is that key? The composer John Cage, whom I once met, could have said: It's in silence. And his collegue, Edgar Varèse, was looking into space to find out which role mankind was playing without grasping the meaning of its quest.

Nevertheless, time passes. When you read this, a century might have gone, two centuries, a million years ... I don't mind. I don't belong to time, that's to say time that has been a time of prison and of disaster. Therefore I still write letters to Shanti, the peace of the world. And what I hear in this space is my composition beyond all times: *Time Zero. Bells in the Wind*.

Percival

www.ingramcontent.com/pod-product-compliance
Lightning Source LLC
Chambersburg PA
CBHW051133020726
47501CB00005B/1494

* 9 7 8 9 1 9 7 3 4 3 4 7 3 *